FROM THE
NANCY DREW FILES

THE CASE: Nancy has to track down the zoo's valuable missing civet cats and clear her friend's boyfriend, who is suspect #1.

CONTACT: George's new boyfriend, zoology student Owen Harris, is blamed for the cats' disappearance.

SUSPECTS: Zoe Spelios—the glamorous French zookeeper and Owen's boss—is too good to be true. What does she have to hide?

Tyler Mack—the assistant zookeeper hates Zoe and loves luxury. Where is he getting all the money he's spending?

Owen Harris—why is the zoo's tranquilizer gun in the trunk of the young scientist's car?

COMPLICATIONS: A tall stranger in sunglasses is unquestionably trying to run Nancy off the trail—permanently.

Books in THE NANCY DREW FILES® Series

Available from ARCHWAY Paperbacks

THE NANCY DREW FILES™ CASE·44

SCENT OF DANGER

Carolyn Keene

AN ARCHWAY PAPERBACK
Published by POCKET BOOKS
New York London Toronto Sydney Tokyo Singapore

AN ARCHWAY PAPERBACK *Original*

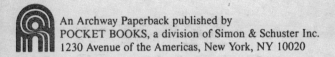

An Archway Paperback published by
POCKET BOOKS, a division of Simon & Schuster Inc.
1230 Avenue of the Americas, New York, NY 10020

ISBN: 0-671-67496-X

First Archway Paperback printing February 1990

10 9 8 7 6 5 4 3 2 1

SCENT
OF DANGER

Chapter

One

OH, THAT SMELL!" Nancy Drew said, wrinkling her nose as she walked into the front hall of her friend George Fayne's house. Sweet, heavy aromas perfumed the air.

George Fayne grinned as she took Nancy's blue and white ski jacket. "It is a little much. You get used to it when you've been inside for a while. I just hope my mom's not sorry she gave Bess permission to have a perfume party at our house."

"I wouldn't worry about it. Bess can be very persuasive," Nancy reminded her, taking off her hat and shaking out her reddish blond hair. She

1

sniffed the air close to George and smiled. "Is that Whisper of Spring you're wearing?"

George reddened. "I know it's a little old and heavy for me, but—"

"Bess can be very persuasive," Nancy finished for her, laughing.

The friends were interrupted by a call from the other room. "George, where did you disappear to? Oh, hi, Nan!" Bess Marvin greeted her friend as she strolled out into the hall. She was waving two perfume atomizers. "Try this, it's really yummy." She pointed the larger bottle at Nancy. "It's called Fantasy."

"Thanks, I think I'll pass," said Nancy, skillfully sidestepping a cloud of spray.

"Me, too," George said, dancing behind Nancy. "I'm fragrant enough as it is."

"Oh, come on, just a little, George. It's perfect for you," Bess said coaxingly.

Nancy, caught between the two girls, laughed as Bess stalked her cousin with the spray bottle. The two girls, cousins and best friends, couldn't have been more different. Bess was all blond hair, blue eyes, and pink organza. Dark-haired George was slender, athletic, and hot-color sweats.

"Okay, okay, I give," George said, holding out her wrist so Bess could spray it. "Let's go back in," she added, leading the way into the living room of the Faynes' modest suburban house.

Bess introduced Nancy to the two other girls who had been invited to try on various scents. A short redhead with freckles named Lauren looked up from the floor at Nancy and smiled.

"I've heard of you," she said. "You're that detective, aren't you?"

Nancy tried not to blush. She took pride in the fact that she'd solved some mysteries in and out of River Heights, but having kids her own age recognize her like some kind of celebrity was a little embarrassing.

"She sure is!" Bess said enthusiastically. "In fact, just last month—"

"Oh, Bess, stop," Nancy interrupted her friend. "Why don't you guys get back to the party?"

"That's a great idea," the other girl, Paula, asserted, looking at her watch. "We've got to be home really soon, and there are at least five more perfumes I want to try."

As Bess, Lauren, and Paula went back to picking up various colored bottles and atomizers, Nancy sat down next to George on a comfortable, overstuffed sofa in a corner of the room. "At least here we're out of the line of spray," George said to her.

"Maybe we should open a window," Nancy suggested.

"Good idea." George jumped up and tugged at the window, letting in a blast of cold air. "Brrr!" She shivered, adjusting the window so it was open only a crack. She turned to Nancy, a concerned expression on her face. "This weather is really hard on the warm-weather animals at the zoo."

"Oh, George, I completely forgot," Nancy said, frowning at her own absentmindedness. "You started your new job!" George had signed up as a volunteer tour guide at the River Heights Zoo. "How's it going?"

"I love it," George answered, her face lighting up. "I'm working at a brand-new exhibit that actually simulates living conditions in the African wild."

"How does it do that?" Nancy asked, fascinated.

"The animals live in totally glassed-in cases that are planted like grasslands and forests. They're temperature controlled. There's even a desert environment," she explained excitedly. "Owen says it's very close to the way they live in the wild."

"It does sound much more humane," Nancy said with a nod.

"That's what Owen says," George agreed.

"So long, Nancy!" Lauren called out. She and Paula were standing in the hallway, putting on their winter coats. "It was great meeting you." Paula pulled her friend out of the doorway, saying, "Come on, we're going to be late."

"Who is this Owen, George?" Bess asked, coming back into the living room. "I notice his name keeps coming up."

"He works at the zoo." Nancy noticed that

George developed a sudden interest in the flowered pattern on the couch. She ran her fingers over it, looking at the couch instead of Bess as she explained. "Actually, he's a college student. He's doing a research project on the behavior of civets."

"What-its?" Bess asked.

"They're sort of like wild cats," George explained. "They live in Africa and Asia."

"Is Owen a zoology major?" Nancy asked.

George nodded. "He was sure he'd have to go to Africa for his civet project, but then the zoo got a special donation to start its own project and he came to River Heights instead. He says he's not too sorry he didn't go to Africa."

"I'll bet he isn't," Nancy teased her friend gently. "He would never have gotten a chance to meet you." George's blush confirmed Nancy's suspicion that Owen wasn't just interested in civets.

"He's pretty cute," George admitted, "and I think he likes me. He always comes over to answer questions when I bring groups around."

"Has he asked you out?" asked Bess, eager for the details.

George shook her head no. "He's only at the zoo a few days a week—the rest of the time he does research in Chicago. He's very serious about his work."

"What a drag," Bess said sympathetically.

"Oh, I don't know," Nancy said. "Ned takes

school very seriously, too. That's part of what I like about him." Ned Nickerson, Nancy's boyfriend, was a student at Emerson College, which meant they only saw each other for vacations and occasional weekends.

"Nancy's right. I wouldn't want a lightweight." She let out a little sigh. "I just wish he had more time to hang out, that's all."

"He'll find time," Bess said comfortingly. "We'll make him!" She rummaged through the box of perfume bottles, coming up with a mysterious dark green flask. "This one's called Temptress. It's absolutely guaranteed to make men fall at your feet." She held it out to her cousin.

George grabbed a magazine off the coffee table and held it in front of her face. "I don't think I want him at my feet," she said from behind her fortress.

"She just wants him at her door." Nancy laughed.

"Oh, well." Bess shrugged, undaunted. "Maybe I'll use a little myself."

"If you had any more men at your feet, you wouldn't be able to walk," George teased. Her curvy cousin was a bit of a temptress herself.

"Maybe I'll attract someone *serious*," she shot back, liberally dabbing herself with the perfume.

George fanned herself with the magazine to clear the air. "Phew! That should bring them running." Her face grew serious. "I doubt it would work on Owen, though. He's got so much on his mind, I'm surprised he notices me at all."

"You mean his project?" Nancy asked.

"Not exactly. In fact, I wanted to talk to both of you about it, but—"

"Go on, George," Bess urged. "What's wrong?"

George paused a moment before continuing. "Some strange things have been going on at the zoo."

"Strange, how?" Nancy asked, puzzled.

"Well, a few days ago two of the civets disappeared," George said.

"You mean they escaped?"

"Some people thought so, but then I heard a rumor that Owen let them out by mistake," George said angrily. "I know that's not true. I'm positive they were stolen!"

Nancy started to ask her friend how she could be so sure, then stopped herself. George obviously believed that Owen could do no wrong. She must really like him, Nancy thought. It wasn't like George to get so emotional.

Bess was more direct. "Why would anyone want to steal the civets?" she asked.

"I-I'm not sure," George said uncertainly. "That's part of what I wanted to talk to you about."

"Maybe Owen did let them out. Anyone can make a mistake," Bess pressed.

"If he'd made a mistake, he would have admitted it," George said defensively. "I think—" The jangle of the telephone interrupted her.

She got up to pick up the phone. "Hello—oh, Owen!" she said, barely containing the excitement in her voice. "How are you?"

Bess raised an eyebrow at Nancy. "I told you the perfume would get him," she whispered. Nancy laughed and shushed her.

Whatever Owen was saying made George smile and blush. Then her friend's expression changed to one of concern. "Not again," George said breathily into the receiver.

Nancy leaned forward. Whatever had happened sounded serious. As George listened quietly to Owen, her expression grew more and more concerned. Finally George hung up with a goodbye and turned back to Nancy and Bess.

"That was Owen," she said. Her voice sounded strained, and she nervously wiped her hands on her pants.

Nancy jumped up and walked over to put a reassuring hand on George's arm. "Tell us what's wrong, George."

George looked into Nancy's eyes. She looked as if she was about to burst into tears. "Oh, Nancy," she said, a catch in her voice. "Two more civets have disappeared, and zoo security now thinks Owen stole them!"

Chapter
Two

"WHY DO THEY THINK Owen would do it?" Nancy asked, calmly trying to cut through George's panic. "What kind of proof do they have?"

George looked angry. "I don't know. I do know one thing for sure—he didn't do it," she said loyally. "If you ask me, it's all one big setup!" She began pacing the room.

Nancy followed her friend with her eyes. It seemed to her that George was letting her emotions run away with her. Thinking that Owen was being framed was a big leap.

"How can you be so sure?" Bess asked, almost

reading Nancy's thoughts. "Maybe the civets escaped on their own."

"That's nearly impossible," George told her. "The glass enclosure has only one door, and it's always locked."

"So what makes you think Owen's being set up? That's a pretty heavy accusation, you know," Nancy pointed out.

"I realize that," George said. "But I think other people are jealous because Owen's project is going so well," she added.

Nancy frowned. "What other people? Other researchers?"

George nodded. "Research can get pretty cut-throat."

"Now that he's been accused, how is Owen going to defend himself?" Bess put in.

"He hasn't been formally accused, so he says he isn't going to defend himself." George looked worried. "He says his reputation should speak for itself." She turned to Nancy. "I'm worried, though. If someone at the zoo is out to get him, his reputation will be ruined. Nancy, I wish you'd look into this."

"That's a great idea!" Bess said enthusiastically. "I'm sure you could figure out who's setting Owen up."

If he *has* been set up, Nancy thought to herself. What if he *was* guilty? If she found evidence against Owen, that could cause a big strain on her friendship with George.

Hiding her misgivings, she said lightly, "I don't know if I'm ready for another case. I'm still recovering from the last one."

"I bet you could solve this in no time," Bess said stubbornly. "I think you ought to try to help Owen."

"I'd really appreciate it," George added.

Nancy raised her hands in surrender. "All right, lead the way." How could she resist the pleas of her two best friends? They were always there when she needed them.

"Thanks!" George said, giving her a quick hug. "Can you come to the zoo with me in the morning?"

"Sure. What time?"

"I'm coming, too," Bess broke in. "I want a look at this guy. Anyone who gets George to put on perfume is worth checking out," she added, poking her cousin in the ribs.

"I have to be there at eight-thirty," George said.

Bess groaned. "On second thought—" Nancy grinned, knowing how much Bess hated to get up early. Bess took a deep breath and announced, "I'll go anyway. You might need moral support."

"That's the Bess I know and love!" said Nancy approvingly. "I'll pick you up at eight."

"Not me," George said. "I might need my car. Bess, could you put that stuff away and open some windows?" George asked, fanning her face.

"The house has to be aired out before my mother gets home."

"The things I do for my friends," Bess grumbled, yawning. "No one should ever have to wake up before ten."

She and Nancy had just pulled into the parking lot of the River Heights Zoo. "You're amazing," Nancy agreed, choosing a spot near the entrance. Bess might complain, but when her friends needed help she always came through.

As Nancy was pulling into the spot, she saw George coming out of the entrance, followed by a blond boy in horn-rimmed glasses. "Look, there's George. She really got here early."

Bess leaned forward, all traces of tiredness gone. "That must be Owen. Hey, he's cute! I'm not crazy about the glasses, but check out his muscles. He looks like he works out."

George recognized Nancy's blue Mustang and waved to her. "You can park in the staff area!" she called, indicating a roped-off section of the lot.

After Nancy parked, she and Bess joined George and Owen by the gate. George introduced everyone. "This is my cousin, Bess Marvin, and Nancy Drew. Bess, Nancy, this is Owen Harris."

"You're the detective, right?" Owen said, raising his eyebrows in disbelief as he shook Nancy's hand.

Bess must have picked up on Owen's expression, because she quickly defended her friend. "Nancy's a very well-known detective. She's never blown a case."

"Really?" Owen said. He looked pointedly at Nancy's jeans and ski jacket. He obviously wasn't convinced. What did he expect, Nancy thought, a Sherlock Holmes outfit?

Nancy found herself liking Owen more as she listened to him talk about his work. "World of Africa is a special exhibit because it considers the animals' needs," he explained, leading them into the building where the exhibit was housed. "For instance, some animals tend to form colonies, while others prefer to live alone. By studying their behavior, zoologists can learn the best way to group them in captivity."

They stopped in front of a large glass cage. Inside was a single chimp. "This is Dibo," Owen said. "Most chimpanzees like to live in family groups, but this one's a loner. His cage has a trapdoor that connects with the rest of the family, so he can choose when he wants company and when he'd rather be by himself."

"Like giving a kid his own room," Bess said, fascinated.

Owen smiled. "Exactly. In monkey years Dibo is about fifteen. He needs his space just like teenagers do."

"You care so much about animals," Nancy commented. Watching how animated his face became as he talked about Dibo, Nancy found it difficult to believe that Owen could have stolen the civets.

Owen nodded. "Always have. I was the kind of kid who brought home lame squirrels. I always wanted to talk to them." He laughed and his eyes twinkled behind the glasses. "I guess being a zoologist is the closest I can get to them."

He led them away from the chimp, stopping to whisper something to George, who smiled up at him. "You should see this place when the zoo's open," she said to Nancy and Bess as they followed him across the large room. "It's packed."

Owen stopped at a glassed-in area about thirty feet square. Inside were some bushes and small trees, which appeared to be flourishing under the fluorescent lights. "This is the civet colony," he explained. "As you can see, it doesn't look anything like a cage."

"Where are the civets?" Nancy asked.

"Most of them are sleeping—up in the trees," Owen told her. "They sleep as much as twenty hours a day."

Suddenly one of the civets leapt from a tree, causing Bess to scream and jump backward. "I forgot there was glass," she said sheepishly as the others turned to her in surprise.

"I think this one is a female," Owen said, pointing to the civet.

"She's adorable," Bess said, having recovered from her fright. To Nancy the civet looked like a large housecat, except that it had an extremely long tail. The cat was tan with black markings. "Sort of like a leopard," Bess commented.

"How many are there?" Nancy asked.

Owen frowned. "There used to be ten, but now we're down to six."

"George explained to us what happened," Nancy told Owen. "Is there any way the civets could have escaped?"

"No way," Owen said firmly. "There's only one door to the exhibit—you can't see it. It's designed to be hidden." Nancy followed the direction of his finger to some bushes near the back of the enclosure. "The door is locked, and it leads to a supply room that's also kept locked."

Nancy mused aloud. "So even if the civet got out of the exhibit, it would be trapped in the supply room."

"That's right. There's also an alarm that rings in the security office whenever anyone enters or leaves the exhibit. You can turn it off, but you need a special key. The security people didn't hear any alarm. That's why they're sure it was a theft."

"And they think you did it," Nancy concluded, turning her back on the exhibit to look hard at Owen.

He shrugged, keeping his eyes on the civets behind the glass. "I work late a lot, and I have the keys, so I'm a natural suspect. Personally, I think that whoever did it is setting me up. The head of security questioned me again last night," he added.

"You don't seem too upset," Nancy commented.

"I didn't do it," Owen said, finally facing Nancy. There was no anger in his voice. "Sooner or later they'll catch the person who did."

"You said someone might be trying to set you up," Bess pressed.

Instead of answering, Owen just shrugged again, as if he were impatient with the whole conversation. Bess exchanged a look with Nancy. Neither of them could understand why Owen was being so evasive. Nancy wondered if it was because he did have something to hide.

George jumped in. "I bet it could be Tyler," she said quickly.

"Who's he?" Nancy asked Owen.

"Tyler Mack. The assistant zookeeper," Owen answered grudgingly. "He's always giving me a hard time."

"He's been really mean to Owen," George confirmed, leaving Bess's side and going to stand next to him.

"That's just his personality. He's mean to everyone," Owen told her. "I don't see why he'd want to steal civets, let alone pin their theft on me."

Nancy was about to ask Owen a question when a pretty, dark-haired woman came up to them. She was wearing a white lab coat, unbuttoned, over a pair of beautifully tailored black pants and a rose-colored sweater. Although the woman was dressed casually, she wore her clothes with a natural elegance.

"Owen, are these your friends?" she asked. Her voice had a slight French accent.

"They're friends of George's," Owen answered. He introduced her as Zoe Spelios, the zookeeper in charge of the Africa exhibit.

"I prefer 'curator,'" Zoe said with a low laugh. "It sounds more artistic, no?"

"Apparently, Nancy is a detective," Owen said, not bothering to keep the skepticism out of his voice. "George thought she could help us find the civets."

The dark-haired woman looked Nancy up and down. "Aren't you a little young to be doing such dangerous work?" she asked, emphasizing the word *dangerous*.

"I've done pretty well so far," Nancy told her. Zoe raised her eyebrows, clearly not believing her.

Without further comment, Zoe excused herself. "I must see to the snake's breakfast," she told Owen. "Please get to work as soon as possible."

"What a chic woman," Bess commented, watching her hurry away.

Owen nodded. "Would you believe that she's a reptile expert, a herpetologist? One of the vipers is sick, and she's trying to get it to eat."

"Well, she looks more like a fashion model than a zookeeper. And she was wearing an absolutely fabulous perfume," Bess said, gushing. "Did you notice, George?"

"You've got perfume on the brain," George answered, teasing her. "Now let's get out of Owen's way so he can get to work," she added.

"I'd like to take a look at the door to the civet room, if you have a minute," Nancy said.

"It's in the back," Owen said. "I have time to show it to you. We'll have to go around the side of the building."

As they were leaving the building, a short red-haired man in a lab coat stopped Owen. "Taking a break already, Harris?" he asked with a sneer.

"Just showing some friends around, Tyler," Owen answered agreeably. "Bess, Nancy, this is Tyler Mack. You already know George, Tyler."

Mack nodded. "Your little girlfriend," he said nastily. George turned red with embarrassment.

Ignoring George, Tyler asked Bess, "Are you girls going to be tour guides, too?"

"Actually, Nancy's a detective," Bess replied, trying to contain her temper. "She's investigating the civet thefts."

Tyler shot Owen a sharp look. "Did Zoe approve this, or is it something you dreamed up on your own?" he asked Owen icily. Not waiting for an answer, he turned to Nancy. "On second thought, I doubt Harris would want an investigation. He's looks pretty guilty right now."

"You can't prove anything!" George said angrily.

"Can't I?" He gave George a withering stare. "Either way, the security people can handle it without interference from amateurs." Tyler looked down his nose at Nancy even though she was taller than he. Then he turned to Owen. "Especially if they're friends of yours."

As Nancy watched, Tyler leaned in to Owen until his face was only a few inches from the student's. He dug his index finger into Owen's chest for emphasis. "You better keep your nose out of this business, Harris. Or I'll personally guarantee you'll be out of here before you know what happened!"

Chapter

Three

W<small>HY, YOU</small>—" His temper finally igniting, Owen stepped menacingly toward the other man, his hands outstretched. "Where do you get off, accusing and threatening me?" he asked angrily.

Nancy gently placed a hand on Owen's arm. "Think about what you're doing, Owen," she said, trying to calm him down.

George took his other arm. "Relax, Owen. It won't help if you lose your temper."

"You better listen to your little friends," Tyler jeered. Before Owen could reply, he turned and stalked away.

Owen balled his hands into fists, and he stared after the man with a look of hatred in his eyes.

"That rat! He'd be happy to see my project go up in smoke."

"Don't let him get to you," George said softly. "He doesn't know what he's talking about."

Owen looked down at George and slowly relaxed his hands. "Sorry about that," he murmured with an apologetic smile. Then he turned to the others. "I don't know what came over me." He shook himself and raked his hands through his sandy blond hair. "When I think of having to give up this project, I get pretty emotional, I guess."

"That's understandable," Bess said, exchanging a look with Nancy.

"Should we proceed to the door to the civet cage?" Nancy asked, trying to change the subject.

"Sure," Owen said. As he led them outside, Nancy couldn't keep her thoughts off the scene she had just witnessed.

Clearly Owen, in spite of his outward calm, was upset and defensive about the missing civets. Otherwise, Tyler Mack couldn't have gotten to him so easily. Meanwhile, why did Mack have such a grudge against Owen?

Nancy's thoughts were interrupted by Bess. "Where are we going?" she asked Owen.

He was leading them around the side of the building, Nancy saw. "The staff entrance is back here. We bring animals in this way, too."

The staff entrance was hidden behind some trees, right next to the parking lot. It would be easy to move animals in, or out, without anybody noticing, Nancy thought.

"What's that?" Bess asked as they were about to go in the staff entrance. She was pointing up in the air.

Nancy looked up and saw a gondola swing by on an aerial cable. "Looks like a new ski lift," she commented.

"That's the Sky Ride," Owen explained. "It gives visitors an aerial tour of the zoo."

"I'd like to take it sometime," George said to him. "The other guides say it's really fun."

"It is," Owen assured her. "I'll take you later, if you want."

"I'd love it," George said, smiling.

Owen used a key to open the staff door. Inside was a reception area with several offices opening off it, and beyond that a long, wide hallway. The hall was lined with doors, each bearing the name of a type of animal.

Owen stopped at the door marked Civets. "This is the back door to the exhibit," he explained. "Through here is a small room where we keep food and supplies, and then the exhibit itself."

He unlocked the door to the supply room, and the others followed him in. Nancy knelt to examine the inner door for signs of a break-in.

Owen turned to Nancy. "Do you see anything strange?"

She nodded. "Depends on your point of view.

22

There aren't any scratches or signs of tampering." She examined it again. "Whoever broke in here was either an extremely skillful lock pick or had a key." She stood up and brushed the dust off her knees. "Can I look on the other side of the door?"

Owen nodded, looking impressed by her deduction. "I'm not supposed to let you, but I guess I can make an exception," he said in a friendlier voice than he'd used before. He put his key in the door and turned the lock.

Before he could open it, however, a voice behind them barked, "What are you doing?" Nancy spun around to find a bearded older man staring angrily at them.

"Who gave you permission to be here?" the older man continued.

Owen stepped forward. "I'm Owen Harris, sir," he said nervously as the man's eyes bored into him. "I'm doing a project on civet behavior, remember? We met at your office last month." He introduced the others to the man. "This is Maurice Berry. He's one of the directors of the zoo."

"Oh, yes, Harris. I've heard about you," Mr. Berry said, frowning. "Who are these girls? You know visitors aren't allowed back here."

"I'm not a visitor," George said, moving over to stand next to Owen. "I'm a tour guide, and these are my friends Bess Marvin and Nancy Drew."

Berry shook his head. "I don't care who you are, you shouldn't be back here," he said ominously. "It's against the rules— Did you say Nancy Drew?" Berry shook his finger at her. "I've heard about you. I'm told you're quite a detective!"

When he saw Nancy's confused look, Berry explained, "Chief McGinnis is a friend of mine, and he's mentioned you more than once." He glanced from Nancy to her friends. "But what are you doing here? You're not investigating a mystery, I hope?"

"Actually, we are." Quickly Nancy explained about the civets.

Berry turned back to Owen. "Does security know about this?" he asked brusquely.

"Yes, sir," Owen replied nervously. "They haven't turned up anything." Nancy noticed that Owen didn't mention that security was suspicious of him.

"So you brought Nancy in? Good work."

"Actually, it was George's idea," Owen said, smiling at her. George's face lit up.

"Well, it was a good one. Do whatever you have to, Nancy. I'll tell Zoe and Tyler to cooperate."

"Thanks, Mr. Berry. I'd appreciate that."

He nodded. "I have to get back to the office, but let me know if you need anything."

As Berry walked away, Owen fit his key into the lock again and opened the door to the civet exhibit itself. Nancy stepped inside, being careful to stay hidden in the trees that camouflaged the door.

The lock on the inside showed no signs of tampering. "Strange," Nancy murmured.

"Do you see anything?" Bess asked anxiously from behind the door.

"Not even a scratch," Nancy told her. She stepped back out, and Owen shut the door and locked it behind her. "If there's nothing else to see, we'll let you get to work," she told him.

"I have to go, anyway," George said, checking her watch. "My first tour is at nine-thirty, and it's almost that now."

Owen walked them back to the staff entrance. "It was nice meeting you," he said politely, opening the door for them. "Thanks for your help, even if you couldn't find anything."

"I don't think I'll give up just yet," Nancy said casually. Was Owen trying to tell her he didn't want her on the case?

He shrugged. "Whatever. Keep at it if you want to. Just don't waste your time." He turned to George. "If you want to have lunch, stop by around one," he told her in a softer voice. George nodded happily, and he brushed her cheek with his hand. "See you then."

Nancy and Bess walked down the path to the parking lot, with George floating behind them in a romantic daze.

"What did he mean, don't waste your time?"

Bess whispered furiously as they passed an outdoor sea lion tank. "He acts as if we're just doing this for fun."

Nancy shrugged. "I guess he doesn't take us seriously." Her casual tone hid the fact that she, too, was a little ticked off by Owen's attitude.

George caught up with them near the gate, in front of a giraffe habitat. "I have to meet a group here in a few minutes," she told them. "So what do you think? Isn't Owen cute?"

"Gorgeous," Nancy said before Bess, who had opened her mouth, could speak. In her current state of bliss, George wasn't going to react kindly to any criticism of Owen. Bess sensed what Nancy was getting at and kept quiet.

"George," Nancy went on, "are you sure Owen wants me on the case?"

Her friend looked shocked at Nancy's question. "Of course he does!" she assured her. "Why?"

"No reason," Nancy told George. "I guess we'd better be going," she said, changing the subject. "I want to check out a few things."

"Like what?" George asked.

"We still don't know what motives the thief might have for stealing the civets," she explained. "Why don't you come over after dinner tonight, and we'll put our heads together?"

"Sounds good. Thanks again for your help, Nancy." George smiled gratefully.

As they drove out of the parking lot, Bess crossed her arms and said, "I don't mind telling you I'm not crazy about Owen. He acts like we're a couple of empty-headed teenagers."

Nancy concentrated as she made a left-hand turn out of the lot into traffic. Then she said, "He doesn't know us."

"So what? We're friends of George's."

"Still, we probably do look like meddling kids to him," Nancy pointed out.

"Mr. Berry didn't think so," Bess said in a satisfied voice. "Owen was pretty surprised that he knew about your detective work."

Nancy nodded. "Did it seem to you that Mr. Berry had something against Owen?" she asked her friend.

Bess thought about it. "He seemed a bit abrupt at first, but that was all," she said finally.

"I wonder," Nancy mused. A little while later she turned the Mustang into the parking lot of the River Heights Mall.

Bess looked at her in surprise. "Nancy, where are we going? Don't tell me you have a sudden urge to shop!"

Nancy laughed. "Sorry, no. I'm just looking for information."

"At the mall?" Bess asked. She eyed her friend as if she'd gone crazy. "What kind of information can you get here?"

"I want to find out if civet fur is at all valuable," Nancy explained. She pulled up outside a store with a big sign in the window that read Hermanovich Furs.

Bess's blue eyes had been sparkling at the thought of going to the mall, but now she looked serious. "Oh, no. You don't think the civets have been made into coats, do you?"

"That's what we're here to find out," Nancy told her.

Nancy parked and the two friends went inside, where they were greeted by a chubby, white-haired man.

"Can I help you girls?" he asked with a twinkling smile. "Maybe something in a nice fur jacket?"

"Actually, I just have a couple of questions," Nancy said.

"If it's about fur, I'm your man. Alexander Hermanovich, furrier," he said proudly.

Nancy introduced herself and Bess, and explained that they were looking for information on civets. "Are their pelts ever used for coats?" she asked.

Mr. Hermanovich shook his head. "I've never heard of one," he said. "Like many wild animals, civets won't breed in captivity. Most fur coats are made from animals like mink and rabbit, which breed easily."

"But if civet fur is rare, wouldn't that make it more valuable?" Bess asked.

"In some cases rarity does increase the value,"

Mr. Hermanovich admitted. "However, because civet fur is extremely coarse, it wouldn't be comfortable." He shook his head. "I doubt that anyone would even want a coat made from civets."

Nancy bit her lower lip. That pretty much ruled out one motive. She thanked Mr. Hermanovich for his help and found Bess.

"At least now we know that the civets probably aren't being stolen for fur," Nancy said as they left the store.

"That's right. So what do we do next?" Bess asked.

"I don't know." Nancy shook her head in frustration. "We're no further along than we were before. We've still got to find a motive for the civet thefts." The girls were standing outside the mall in the winter sunshine.

"While we're thinking about it, how about an early lunch? Something nice and fattening?" Bess asked. "I don't know about you, but I have trouble solving cases on an empty stomach."

"What about that five pounds you've been threatening to lose," Nancy said, teasing her.

Bess's eyes grew round, and Nancy knew Bess was trying to come up with an excuse for abandoning her diet. Bess looked great, but she constantly struggled with losing the same five pounds she had decided would make her perfect.

Bess opened her mouth, her excuse obviously rehearsed and ready. Before she could launch into it, she stopped herself. "Nancy, what's that man doing to your car?"

A man in jeans and a ski jacket was crouched down beside Nancy's Mustang. Motioning Bess to stay back, Nancy edged up behind a neighboring car and peered at him around it.

The man appeared to be doing something to the Mustang, but Nancy was still too far away to see exactly what. Cautiously she came out from behind the car and made her way directly toward him.

When she was a few yards from her car, Nancy was able to get a better look at what the man was doing. To her dismay, she saw he had a lock-pick in his hands. He was breaking into her car!

Chapter

Four

ALTHOUGH SHE REMAINED perfectly still, Nancy's mind was racing. If this was a simple car robbery, the thief was taking a big chance attempting it in broad daylight. The man must have some other motive for breaking into her car.

As she kept an eye on him, Nancy started to plan her strategy. She didn't necessarily want to scare him away. Better to wait, she decided, to find out exactly what he did want.

Then Nancy heard Bess coming up behind her. She motioned her friend to keep back, but Bess let out an involuntary gasp when she saw what the man was up to.

Hearing the noise, the man jumped to his feet

31

and spun around. Now that her cover was blown, Nancy stepped forward and said firmly, "What are you doing to my car?"

"It's your car? I thought it was mine," the man said with a heavy accent. His mirrored sunglasses made it impossible for Nancy to read his expression. She did notice, however, that the tall, thin stranger had palmed his lock-pick tool and was now innocently dangling a set of car keys.

"You bet it is," Nancy said. "What I want to know is—"

Before Nancy could finish her sentence, the man was sprinting across the parking lot.

"Hey! Stop him!" Bess called out. The few shoppers straggling across the lot stopped to look at Bess, but the man was already around the corner of the mall.

"That was totally bizarre," Nancy commented. She searched the lot for some sign of the man, but he had completely disappeared. Nancy shook her head in confusion, then climbed into the Mustang. Bess was already buckled into the passenger seat.

"Do you think he really thought this was his car?" Bess asked as Nancy started the ignition.

"I don't know. It doesn't seem likely," Nancy said. She drove out of the mall and pulled onto the main road. "Not likely at all," she repeated, glancing in the rearview mirror. "Especially since his car is a van."

"What?" Bess looked confused.

"Check out the green van behind us. Isn't that the same guy?"

"It is!" Bess grabbed the armrest as Nancy took a sudden right. When Bess looked back, the man was still behind them.

No doubt about it—he was following them, Nancy knew.

A fast plan formed in her mind. At the next intersection, she made a sharp U-turn and doubled back.

"He's still with us," Bess reported, glancing behind her.

"Hang on, I'm going to try to lose him. Then maybe we can follow *him*—maybe we can find out who he is," she explained when Bess gave her a confused look.

With Bess clutching the edge of her seat, Nancy made two more quick turns and cut through an alley. When she came back onto the street, the van was nowhere in sight.

"I think the alley was too narrow for him," Bess said breathlessly. "We almost didn't make it ourselves."

Nancy nodded. "Keep an eye out for him. He's got to be around here somewhere."

They circled the area near the mall twice, but didn't see the van. "I guess we lost him," Nancy said at last with a disappointed sigh.

"What do you think he wanted?" Bess wondered. "Hey—maybe it had something to do with the missing civets!"

Nancy smiled. Bess had a knack for jumping to conclusions. "It could be anything, Bess. At this point there's no way of knowing."

Bess shook her head slowly. "I don't know, Nancy. I get the feeling there's more to this case than a simple theft," she said.

"If there is, we'll find out soon enough," Nancy told her. "In the meantime, let's go have a big sandwich—and a milkshake—on me."

That evening the doorbell rang just as Nancy and her father, Carson Drew, were finishing dinner.

"Expecting someone, Nancy?" Mr. Drew asked.

"It's probably George," she answered, jumping up. "She said she'd come by after dinner."

George came in, stamping her feet and blowing on her fingers.

"Come on in and warm up," Nancy invited her. "We're just having dessert."

"Did I come too early? I had a hamburger with Owen after work and then came straight here."

"You're not early—unless you don't like chocolate mousse," Nancy assured her. "Hannah left some for us before she went off to visit her sister." Hannah Gruen was the Drews' longtime housekeeper.

"If Hannah made it, it's got to be good,"

George said, unzipping her coat and handing it to Nancy. "Is Bess here yet?"

"She's not coming," Nancy said. "She called about an hour ago to say she had a date with a hunk." Nancy raised her eyebrows and smiled. "She felt bad, but I guess she couldn't resist."

"Her latest football player, I guess." George laughed and followed Nancy into the dining room. "Hi, Mr. Drew."

"Hi, George." Carson Drew looked up, and his handsome face creased into a smile. "Nancy's been telling me about your job at the zoo. Are you enjoying it?"

"It's wonderful," George said eagerly, nodding her thanks as Nancy made her a bowl of the chocolate dessert. "My groups are mostly little kids, and they ask the greatest questions! Today one boy asked me what penguins look like without their tuxedos on."

"What did you tell him?" Nancy asked, grinning.

"Before I could answer, the girl next to him said, 'They look the same, dummy, only naked!'"

Nancy and her father laughed. "It sounds like fun," Carson said. "I wish I could stay and hear more about it, but unfortunately I have to be in court early tomorrow, and I still have a bit more work to do." He stood up, then bent over to kiss his daughter on the forehead. "Good night, Nancy. Nice seeing you, George."

"You too, Mr. Drew." After he left, George

turned to Nancy with a gleam in her eye. "Okay. What do you think of him?"

"George, I love my dad, you know that!" Nancy hid a smile while George let out a groan.

"Not your father, dummy. Owen!" George poked her in the ribs.

"Ohhh—Owen," she said innocently. She had been expecting George's question and had already chosen her words. "He's obviously very intelligent. And he really seems to care about animals."

"Oh, he does. He knows more about them than anyone I've ever met." George's face lit up as she talked. "He knows about all kinds of things, Nancy, but he's not at all boring about them."

She smiled shyly and continued, "Like tonight at dinner. I could have listened to his stories for hours, but he wanted to hear about me. You know what he said? He likes it that I'm an athlete. He says that's probably why I walk so gracefully." She blushed a little at the memory.

Suddenly she pushed away her dessert. "But I won't walk gracefully if I eat all this! I'll waddle."

"One dish of mousse won't do you in," Nancy told her. "But if you're done, let's go sit in the living room."

Nancy and George headed into the living room where George continued to talk about Owen. Nancy flopped onto the sofa to listen to her friend.

"The thing is, I can't believe he really likes me!" George said. She was sitting sideways on a big, comfortable chair with her legs thrown over one arm. "I mean, I'm not like Bess. I don't wear nail polish that matches my lipstick——"

"You don't have to," Nancy told her, smiling at the thought of George in matching lipstick and nail polish. "You look super without frills."

George nodded. "I guess so. I'm not putting myself down. Usually I do think I'm pretty good, but I never guessed I'd be dating someone as neat as Owen. We're going out again tomorrow night," she added.

"Things seem to be happening awfully fast," Nancy said simply, trying not to color her comment.

"I know, isn't it great?" George's voice rose as her level of excitement did. "I feel like this could be something special."

Nancy didn't answer. George was obviously crazy about Owen. Unlike Bess, who'd had dozens of boyfriends, George had only fallen for a handful of guys. Could she tell the difference between a boy who really cared for her and one who was just playing around?

"Nancy, are you listening?" George's voice cut through Nancy's thoughts. "I asked if you thought I should get a haircut."

"Your hair looks great," Nancy said automatically. "Really, *you* look great," she added warmly. "Romance is good for you." Give it a rest, Drew, she scolded herself. George is happy and excited, and there's no reason to spoil it for her.

George was standing in front of the mirror, combing her hair into a different style. Suddenly she turned to Nancy, a stricken expression on her face. "I can't believe I forgot to ask you. Where did you go this afternoon? Did you find out anything?"

"A couple of things." Nancy told her about their visit to the furrier. She also mentioned the man who had followed them.

George was worried. "I wonder what he was doing to your car? I hope I haven't gotten you involved in anything risky," she added, an expression of concern clouding her face.

"Well, we didn't have any trouble losing him, so he's probably not a professional," Nancy said. Before she could continue she was interrupted by the doorbell.

"I wonder who that can be? It's nine o'clock," George said.

Nancy shrugged and headed for the front door as the buzzer rang again. George went with her to the door. When she opened it, Owen was standing outside.

"Owen! Is anything wrong?" Nancy asked. He was pale, she noticed, under the porch light.

"Are you all right?" George asked with concern.

"Yes, fine." He ran his hands through his hair. "I went to your house first, and your mom said you were here." Ignoring Nancy, he grabbed George by the shoulders.

"Another civet is missing—and this time I know someone's trying to frame me!"

Chapter

Five

WHY IS THIS HAPPENING to you?" George moaned. She went onto the porch and tenderly ran her fingers down his cheek.

Owen impetuously hugged George close. "I don't know," he murmured softly in her hair.

Nancy stood inside the hall while George clung to Owen. After a few seconds she cleared her throat. "Um, why don't you come in, Owen? It's freezing out there," she added.

Owen pulled away from George and remained standing on the porch. "I can't. I'm sorry," he told George tenderly. "I just want to get home and get some sleep—try to forget everything for the rest of the night."

"What can we do to help?" George asked. "You can't stand by and let someone ruin your project. Your career, even."

"Why don't we meet at the zoo early tomorrow," Owen said. "We can talk about it then."

"Is eight o'clock all right?" George asked. Owen nodded. "Nancy, can you make it then?"

"I can if Owen wants me to," Nancy said. She caught him shrugging ever so slightly in George's direction.

But George was looking at Nancy and didn't notice. "Of course he does. Don't you?" she asked him.

"Uh—sure. Well, see you then, Nancy," Owen replied. He smiled at George. "I'll see you then, too, beautiful." He gave George a peck on the cheek and with a wave was halfway down the walk to his car.

"He called me beautiful and kissed me!" George exclaimed after Nancy shut the door. She waltzed around the room with an invisible partner. "Am I going to have sweet dreams tonight!"

Nancy watched her friend, lost in thought. Owen definitely knew how to put on the charm when he chose. Still, someone apparently had disliked him enough to try to pin the blame for the missing civets on him.

Nancy frowned as she had another thought. Why was Owen so positive it was a setup? And why did he seem so reluctant to have Nancy involved? Was he afraid she might stumble on something that would actually implicate *him?* Nancy fervently hoped her theory wasn't true. Otherwise, she'd destroy George's newfound happiness.

Nancy left a message for Bess on the Marvins' answering machine early the next morning before heading off to the zoo. When Nancy arrived, she found Owen and George waiting for her in Owen's office.

"Nancy! You're just in time," George greeted her. "Owen was just going to tell me the details of last night."

"Then I won't interrupt." Nancy nodded to Owen, who muttered a greeting. "Please go on."

Owen explained, "The whole thing was really weird. I went back to the zoo after dinner to finish up some paperwork. When I was done, I decided to check on the civets before I left. I do it every night—sort of to tuck them in." He blushed a little at the admission, and Nancy decided Owen had a sweet, sensitive side to him.

He continued, "I opened the door to the exhibit. The civets all know me well, and all six usually come out when I stop by. But last night there were only five!"

"Did you look for the other civet?" Nancy asked.

Owen looked annoyed at the question. "Of course I did. I checked the whole exhibit."

Ignoring his irritation, Nancy pressed on. "When was the last time you saw it?"

"Right before dinner," Owen said. "George helped me feed the civets before I left."

"There definitely were six, then?" Nancy prodded.

Owen nodded. "The missing one is the female. I would have noticed if she was missing earlier."

"So the theft must have taken place while you were at dinner," Nancy mused.

"Or after he got back," George pointed out.

"That would have been tough," Owen said. "I was working in my office with the door open. I would have seen anyone sneaking past." He frowned. "Anyway, I just know the whole thing has to be a setup."

Now was the time, Nancy decided, to ask why Owen was so sure he was being framed. "What makes you so positive?" Nancy asked pointedly.

Owen ran a hand through his hair, which looked as if he hadn't combed it that morning. "When I left for dinner, it would have been obvious to anyone I was coming back. I left the lights on, and my stuff was all over. Why didn't the thief just wait until I'd gone home for the night?"

"What difference would it have made?" George asked, puzzled.

Owen explained, "When you go home, you sign out with the night guard. Since I knew I was coming back, I didn't sign out when we left for dinner."

"So no one but the guard and George knew that you had left the grounds," Nancy commented. "Still, the guard could give you an alibi."

"If he remembers," Owen said. "A lot of people go in and out—that's why they keep the book."

"Even if the guard doesn't remember you, you have an alibi. You were with me," George reminded him.

"Sure, you'd back me up. But is anyone going to believe you?" Owen looked skeptical. "Everyone knows we're friends. You could be lying to defend me."

Nancy had another idea. "What about zoo security? Didn't you call them when you saw the civet was gone?"

Owen looked agitated. "Yeah, I called them. But you know what? They already knew about it."

"How did they know?" George asked.

"They said they had just gotten an anonymous phone call. They were on their way over to check it out. They decided to hold off until morning, though."

Nancy bit her lip. "That's strange that someone else reported it before you did. Still, it's a good thing he or she did. It proves someone knew about the theft. It's also good you called. It could help prove you had nothing to do with it." She glanced around Owen's office. "Was anything different after the theft? Anything moved around?"

"I don't think so." Owen thought for a moment. "Wait a minute. I did notice something strange. The thief took some civet food and supplies."

Nancy pounced. "That means whoever stole the civets has to be keeping them alive." She was about to go on when the door opened and Zoe Spelios stormed in.

The zookeeper was obviously in a bad mood. "I got a call last night about the missing civet, Owen," she said shortly. "Security has some questions for you. They'll be here in a few minutes, so you'd better get rid of your friends."

Then she noticed Nancy. "Maurice Berry told me about you," she said, suddenly very sweet and friendly. "If there's any way I can help you, let me know."

"I'd like to wait here and talk with the security guards, if that's all right," Nancy said.

Zoe hesitated. "Uh—of course." She smiled again. "Whatever you want to do is fine."

The guards arrived a moment later. There were two of them: a young guy, obviously an assistant, and a white-haired man with a beard.

"Harper Anderson," the white-haired man

said, introducing himself. "And this is Art Fine." He turned to Owen. "You must be Owen Harris."

Owen nodded, and Harper asked him to describe what had happened the night before. Then he asked to see the entrance to the civet exhibit.

Owen led them down the long hallway to the door of the exhibit. Nancy, George, and Zoe followed.

Harper stood back and let his assistant examine the locks. Then the two men spoke privately in a corner.

"It doesn't look as if anyone's tampered with it," Harper announced finally. "Which could suggest it's an inside job." He turned to Zoe. "Who has keys to the exhibit?" he asked.

"Just Owen, me, and Tyler Mack," Zoe answered knowingly. "Tyler's my assistant."

Harper nodded. "I know him." He twirled the points on his mustache while he thought for a minute. "Well, Art will dust for prints, and we'll get back to you with the results."

"You mean fingerprints?" Owen asked, his eyes wide. "But I was the last one to touch the door. I came in after dinner last night to check on the civets," he explained, looking at George as if for help.

"That's when he discovered one was missing," George confirmed. "He told us about it afterward."

"Did you call security?" Zoe asked.

Owen shrugged helplessly. "Yes, but—"

"Someone else had called earlier," Harper finished for him.

"We'll be speaking with you soon, Ms. Spelios," he continued, tipping his cap. "And you, young man, watch what you do," he warned, using his index finger to emphasize his point.

Zoe walked with the guards to the main door, then returned to the hall where the others were still gathered. Ignoring Nancy and George, she asked Owen to come into her office.

With a slight shrug to the others, Owen followed Zoe down the hall to an office across from his own. "We can wait in Owen's office," George suggested quietly as they followed the other two back down the hall.

"In a minute." Zoe had left her office door partly open. Motioning George to keep silent, Nancy moved close enough to hear the conversation.

"I have nothing against you personally," Zoe was saying. "It's just that World of Africa is a very expensive project, and we can't afford to have problems."

Nancy moved over to make room for George, who was standing next to her.

"The project was going so well up until now, Zoe," Owen protested. "You know I'm not doing anything wrong and that I care about the civets."

"I know." The zookeeper paused. "In fact,

Tyler says the more involved you get with World of Africa, the more critical you've become about the way things are run."

Nancy leaned forward, frowning at the zookeeper's accusation.

"I've criticized the way *Tyler* runs things," Owen replied. "He's not a responsible—"

"Tyler's not the problem," Zoe said, interrupting him. "I'm giving you a chance to tell your side. Right now you do look like our number-one suspect. So, would you like to explain, Owen?"

Nancy and George moved closer to the office door. Inside, Nancy could see the zookeeper's bookshelves, which contained stacks of papers and books. Zoe Spelios had made an effort to add a personal touch to the office. Next to a framed diploma resting on the shelves was a vase of fresh wildflowers. Beside the vase was a photograph of a handsome older man with a handlebar mustache.

"But that's ridiculous!" Owen was shouting, bringing Nancy back to his conversation with Zoe. "You know what the research from this project means to me! You can't do this!"

"I can and I will," the zookeeper said calmly. "No single project is as important as the good of the whole zoo."

"But I told you, I *care* about the zoo, and I haven't done anything wrong!"

Nancy pulled George back out of sight as Zoe

stood up from her desk. "I can't be sure about that," she heard the zookeeper tell Owen.

"You've got to believe me," Owen insisted, his voice rising in panic.

"I'm sorry, Owen," Zoe went on in a cold, businesslike tone. "Until this thing is resolved, I just can't let you work with the civets anymore. Pack your things. I want you out of here within the hour."

Chapter

Six

"Wh-what?" Owen sputtered. "That's completely unfair!"

Nancy cast a quick look around the doorway to see Owen leaning on Zoe's desk. The zookeeper was standing with her hands on her hips.

"We've got to do something," George whispered. Nancy put her finger to her lips and turned back to watch Zoe.

"You heard me, Owen," the woman was saying. "You can use the research facilities at the main building, but I don't want you in this exhibit hall anymore."

"But—"

"No *buts*. Just clean out your office and go." Nancy jumped back as the zookeeper strode out of her office, with Owen following. "And take your friends with you!" she called back before heading down the hall to the animal enclosures.

George ran to Owen. He looked dazed. "Did you hear that?" he asked in a hollow voice. "My whole project down the drain."

"We'll think of something," George said, determined. "They can't keep you away from your project. They just can't."

Owen took off his glasses and rubbed his eyes. "I can't believe this is happening. My project was going along so well."

Nancy saw a look of utter helplessness pass over Owen's face before he put his glasses back on. "Don't worry, Owen," George told him. "With Nancy on the case we'll find out who did it."

Owen snorted. "We'd better, or else I'm going to have to tell my adviser I was booted off my project on suspicion of theft. If that happens, I may as well forget about graduate school forever."

Once again Nancy found herself distrusting Owen. She knew he cared about the civets, but he seemed to care more about what their disappearance was doing to his reputation. Still, for George's sake, she had to try to help him out.

"Why don't we grab a soda? We can pick one

another's brains about who the thief might be," Nancy explained when Owen and George gave her a curious look.

"That's a great idea," George said. "You can come back afterward and clean out your desk."

Owen smiled and took George's hand. Nancy followed them to the front of the building and back inside.

"Is the zoo snack bar all right?" Owen called back to her.

"Fine," she answered, watching out the window as the first visitors of the morning streamed in. Everything looked so tranquil and normal. No one could have guessed that a thief was taking civets from the zoo. What could possibly be the motive? Why civets? Nancy was stumped. What could be so important about a civet that a person would risk stealing them?

Nancy shook her head, trying to clear her thoughts. A flash of silver caught her eye. Nancy looked outside, trying to pinpoint where it was coming from. She traced it to a man in mirrored sunglasses. It was the same man who had tried to break into her car the day before! As Nancy watched, the man glanced around, then went in the main entrance of World of Africa.

"All right if I join you in a minute?" Nancy said to Owen and George as she took off. She tried to speak casually, even though her heart was racing. "There's something I want to check out."

"Sure," Owen said, and George smiled gratefully. George thinks I'm leaving so she'll have time alone with Owen, Nancy realized.

She winked at her friend, then turned back and hurried into World of Africa. It was a weekday morning, and the exhibit hall echoed with the shouts of kids on school trips. Nancy worked her way through the crowd, finally spotting her quarry in front of the civets.

He was a tall man, with dark hair and olive-colored skin. Nancy guessed he was about thirty years old. That day, instead of jeans, he was wearing an expensive-looking suit.

As she watched, the man stared at the five remaining civets for about five minutes. Then he turned and made his way swiftly to the outside door.

Nancy trailed the man outside and around to the staff door, where he let himself in with a key. That's funny, Nancy thought. Zoe said that only she, Owen, and Tyler had keys to this entrance!

Pausing only a few seconds to let the man get inside, Nancy ran up and managed to catch the handle just before the door swung shut.

Inside, the staff reception area and long hallway were empty. Nancy thought she saw a movement at the far end of the hallway, near the entrance to the civet exhibit.

Her heart pounding, Nancy stole down the

hall. What if she was on the trail of the thief!

As she passed Zoe's office, Nancy thought she heard two voices. One of them definitely was Zoe's; the other belonged to a man.

Nancy had to make a quick decision. She looked down the hall. No sign of the movement she'd seen before. The male voice coming from inside Zoe's office could very well be the man in the sunglasses, she reasoned.

A door right next to Zoe's office, marked Authorized Personnel Only, helped Nancy make up her mind. Thinking she could hear better from in there, she tried the door, which was unlocked. Nancy felt a steely hand come down on her shoulder as she pulled on the door.

"If it isn't Harris's little friend!" said a harsh, unpleasant voice.

Nancy struggled to get free as the hand tightened its grip. She twisted around and found herself staring into Tyler Mack's eyes.

"You really should be more careful, you know," Mack said in a cold voice. He gestured to the door Nancy had her hand on. "Do you know what's inside? It's a holding room for sick or"— he smiled nastily—"vicious animals. Right now there's a rare African cobra in there. Its bite could kill you in an instant."

"I didn't know—" Nancy began.

"Of course not. You couldn't. It's so typical of how this place is run!" Mack said angrily.

"Is that so, Tyler?" Zoe had come out of her

office, carefully closing the door behind her. She gave Tyler an icy stare.

Tyler looked nervous. "I just meant—"

"I know what you meant. It burns you up that I'm the boss, doesn't it?" Then Zoe noticed Nancy. "What are you doing here?"

Before Nancy could reply, Tyler cut in. "Courting disaster. She was about to open the holding room when I found her."

Zoe gasped. "You could have been killed!"

"Isn't that door supposed to be locked?" Tyler challenged. "That's the kind of bad management I'm talking about."

Zoe turned red and clenched her fists in anger. "Get back to work, Tyler," she said finally, "before I do something I regret."

"Like what?" Mack asked. His nervousness was gone, and now he was acting like the aggressor. "You can't fire me, and you know it!"

"Don't push your luck!" she said, lashing out at him. She turned to Nancy. "I know Mr. Berry said you could come back here, but from now on, please call before you come."

"All right." Nancy nodded. There was no point in arguing, she realized—tempers were running too high. Why were Zoe and Tyler so antagonistic? she wondered.

"Now, if you don't mind, I'm in the middle of some important business. Tyler, show Ms. Drew out," Zoe instructed him as she went back into her office and closed the door.

Tyler muttered something under his breath as he walked Nancy to the door. He silently pushed it open for her, then pulled it shut with a resounding slam.

Nancy stared at the locked door for a second and considered waiting around until the man with the sunglasses came out. She decided to get back to George and Owen, who would probably be worried about her by now. She could watch out the window for the man in sunglasses—he'd have to pass that way again.

When she got to the snack bar, George and Owen were sitting at a corner table, talking in low voices. They hardly seemed to notice she'd been gone.

"Is this seat taken?" Nancy asked jokingly, pointing to a chair next to them.

"Oh, Nan, hi!" George blushed as she looked up from what was obviously an intimate conversation. "Owen was just telling me about his school." She gave her friend a puzzled look. "Are you all right, Nan? You look a little shook up."

Nancy said, "I'm okay, but I just had a run-in with Tyler and Zoe." She described her encounter with the two zookeepers.

When she was finished, Owen said, "I knew Tyler was jealous of Zoe—he's made several comments about wanting her job. The weird thing is, for two people who can't stand each other, they spend a lot of time together."

Nancy leaned forward. "What do you mean?"

"You know, after work and stuff. I've seen him follow her out a couple of times, and once I ran into them together at the snack bar."

"I wonder why," Nancy mused. "There's definitely no love lost between them."

"It could be about the exhibit," George said. "After all, they need to work together."

"But why would Tyler have told Zoe she couldn't fire him?" Owen wondered. "I thought she could do whatever she wanted."

"There's more to this than—" Nancy broke off as a glint of silver flashed outside the snack bar. "There he goes! That's the man I saw earlier."

"What man?" asked George, confused.

"The one who followed Bess and me yesterday. I've been waiting for him." Nancy jumped up. "I have to follow him."

"We'll come, too," George said quickly. Owen threw some money on the table for their soda, and the three of them left the snack bar.

The man in sunglasses had turned onto a walkway. They followed him, careful to keep their distance.

"Do you know where this path leads?" Nancy asked Owen.

"To the parking lot, I think," he said. Sure enough, a few minutes later they came out in a field of cars.

The man was hurrying across the lot. When he got into his car, Nancy saw it was the same green van he had driven the day before.

"I'm going to tail him," she told George and Owen. She ran for her car, with the other two right behind her.

The blue Mustang was parked on the other side of the lot, near the street exit. As she came up to it, Nancy saw that she was hemmed in by another car.

"Rats! Someone's double-parked, blocking me in," she called to George, who was running to catch up with her.

"We can take my car," George called back. Without breaking stride, she doubled back to it.

Nancy followed. She was almost across the lot when she saw the van in the distance.

It backed out, spun around, and began to pick up speed. George looked around and gave a frightened scream.

"Nancy, look out!"

Nancy watched as the green van came speeding straight for her!

Chapter

Seven

GEORGE SCREAMED AGAIN. Nancy's leg muscles tightened, and she sprang into action. Instinctively she darted to the left.

But when Nancy looked up again the van had swerved and was still aimed straight at her. It kept coming. Owen and George were too far away to do anything but watch in horror.

Desperate, Nancy dropped and rolled between two parked cars just as the van passed. Its tires sent grit flying at Nancy's face.

When Nancy heard the van roar off and fade in the distance, she exhaled the breath she'd been holding. Her breathing came in ragged gasps. George and Owen rushed over to her.

"Are you hurt?" George's face was pale.

"Nothing broken." Nancy crawled out from between the cars, wincing a little at a pain in her leg. She must have pulled a muscle when she threw herself out of the van's way.

"That was some move," Owen said with admiration. "But I think you should stop working on this case," he said grimly. "I appreciate your wanting to help out, but it's getting too dangerous. That guy wasn't kidding around—he tried to kill you."

"I'm sorry I ever asked you," George added.

"Don't be," Nancy replied with a faint smile. George didn't look reassured. "Besides," Nancy pointed out, "it's too late for me to quit the case now. The guy with the sunglasses obviously thinks I'm involved, so he'd keep trying to get me no matter what."

"You could leave town," Owen suggested.

Nancy shook her head. "Look, this isn't the first time I've been involved in something dangerous."

"*That's* the world's biggest understatement." George smiled, and Nancy smiled back as she remembered all the cases they'd worked on together.

"So don't worry," Nancy told her friend. "If it makes you feel better, I'll take it easy for the rest of the day. I thought I'd call Bess and fill her in on everything," she added.

"I don't think you'll need to call her," George said, looking past Nancy. "Here she is now."

Nancy turned around to see Bess pulling into the parking lot. She drove up to Nancy, George, and Owen and rolled down her window. "Hey, guys! I got your message, Nan," she said. She turned and looked at George, giving her a big, knowing grin and nodding in Owen's direction.

George smiled back at her cousin, who had gotten out of the car and was stomping her feet now to stay warm. "Wait till you hear what you missed. Tell her, Nancy."

Within a few minutes Nancy had filled Bess in on the reappearance of the man in the sunglasses.

"That's really creepy." Bess was quiet for a moment. "It seems to point more and more to his having something to do with the missing civets," she said.

Nancy bit on her lower lip. "Well, we don't have any proof. In fact we don't even know *why* the civets are missing. I'm totally stumped, I admit it, but I do agree. He has something to do with the civets—but what?"

"Look, Nancy," Owen said. "Why don't we all meet later this afternoon, after I clean out my desk? Together we might come up with some real answers."

"That sounds good," George said excitedly. "We use that technique all the time, don't we, Nan?"

61

Nancy grinned. "Maybe with what he knows about civets, Owen can help us figure out why they've got so much appeal for our thief."

"I'm glad that's settled," Bess said. "Does that mean you're up for a trip to the mall?"

"Shopping?" Nancy groaned. "After what I've just been through?"

"There's no better cure." Bess went around to the passenger side of her car and held the door open for Nancy. "Hop in."

The last thing Nancy wanted to do when she was on a case was take time out for shopping, but Bess was a faithful friend. "Oh, all right," she said, "but it had better be fast."

Bess smiled at her friend. "It will be. I just have to return some of the perfume we didn't use at my party to Ms. Willert, the woman who helped me set up the party. It won't take more than a few minutes."

"Do you want me to come with you?" George asked as Nancy got in Bess's car. She glanced at Owen. "I told Owen I'd wait for him while he cleaned out his desk, but . . . " She left the sentence hanging.

Nancy shook her head. "No, go ahead. We'll be fine. Call us at Bess's house later. We can arrange a time and place to meet." She waved goodbye to Owen and George as Bess pulled out of the parking lot.

The two friends were quiet all the way to the mall. Nancy was enjoying the warmth of the car after standing out in the cold for so long. Bess pulled into a spot, and she and Nancy darted into Daly's, a large department store. Daly's had everything, not to mention really good sales.

"What a *fabulous* dress!" Bess screamed as they entered Daly's. She pointed to an off-the-shoulder black velvet gown, with a tight bodice and flaring skirt. "I wonder what I could wear it to?"

Before Nancy could answer, Bess darted off to a counter with a display of jewelry. "Doesn't this bracelet look great with my outfit?" she asked, holding up a chunky silver band. She tried it against her royal blue sweater dress, and the effect was devastating. "I've got to have it. It costs a fortune, but maybe they do layaway."

With difficulty, Nancy dragged her away. "I thought we didn't come to shop."

"Okay, okay," Bess said with a petulant frown. She led the way to a perfume counter. "Is Ms. Willert here?" she asked the saleswoman.

"She's in her office, on the mezzanine," the woman replied, pointing out the escalator to the mezzanine.

Ms. Willert was waiting by the door of her office. She was an elegant woman whose almost white blond hair was swept up in a perfect French knot. Her tailored olive-colored suit had funky, boxy trousers instead of a slim skirt, and a multicolored silk scarf pulled the whole outfit together.

"Can I help you? Why, it's Bess Marvin!" she answered her own question. "How did your party go?"

"Great, thanks," Bess told her. "Although it got a little overpowering by the end." She explained to Nancy, "Ms. Willert helped me set up the perfume party."

"It was a wonderful idea," Ms. Willert praised her. "But call me Felicity, please. Someday you ought to go into promotion, Bess," Felicity said.

"Do you think so?" Bess asked eagerly.

"I started out as a salesperson. Now look at me, running the whole department!" Ms. Willert let out a soft, low laugh. "Anything can happen."

"You must know a lot about perfume," Nancy said.

"It's my passion," Ms. Willert admitted. "No matter how hard I work, I never get bored with new fragrances. Take this one, for example. I think you'll love it, Bess." She took a tray of vials out of a locked drawer and held one up. Light shone through the tiny blue bottle, showing the amber, highly concentrated liquid inside.

"Can I try it on?" Bess asked, the excitement growing in her voice.

"Of course." Felicity Willert pulled out the crystal stopper and placed a drop on Bess's wrist.

"That's heaven!" Bess said, holding up her arm for Nancy to smell.

"It is," Nancy agreed. "What gives it that special smell?"

Felicity smiled knowingly. "A lot of things. Essence of rare wildflowers, the bark of trees found only on certain tropical islands. What makes the scent last, though, is a special oil that's very hard to find."

"Why is it so hard to find?" Nancy asked.

"Because it can only be taken in small quantities from an African animal."

Bess was busy sniffing her wrist, but something Felicity said made Nancy think.

"What animal is that?" she asked.

Felicity Willert gave Nancy a curious look. "A civet, actually. Why do you ask?"

Chapter

Eight

A CIVET?" NANCY ECHOED. "Bess, listen. Felicity just told me that civet oil is used in perfume."

Bess looked up. "You're kidding!"

"Not at all," Felicity said with a smile. "Hardly any perfumes are made with civet oil. It's very hard to get, but very desirable. It makes fragrances keep their full scent longer. Perfumes made with plant oils tend to fade."

Nancy felt they had their first real clue. What if the thief had taken the civets so he could sell their oil on the black market? "How hard is it to find civet oil?" she asked.

Felicity thought for a moment. "I doubt it's too hard. Like most things involving the making of perfume, though, it can be expensive. That's why most perfume companies don't use it."

"I don't get it," Bess said. "How do you get oil from the civet?"

"That you'd have to ask someone who knows about civets," Felicity said. "I'd love to answer all your questions, girls, but I'm afraid I have to get back to work."

"Of course," Nancy said. "Thank you for your time."

"And for these," Bess added, pulling two full bottles of perfume from her purse. "They were left over, and I thought you'd want them back."

"Thank you, Bess," Felicity said, taking them from her. "If there's anything else I can help you with, let me know." She walked Nancy and Bess out of her office and to the top of the escalator. "Take care," she said.

"Isn't she a wonderful woman?" Bess asked as they went down. "Nancy?"

"Hmm . . . " Nancy turned around to face her friend.

"You weren't listening. Were you thinking about the civet oil?"

"Uh-huh," Nancy said, facing the front again and letting her eyes travel over the first floor of the department store. "It could be an important clue— Hey, Bess, look over there." She pointed to a nearby counter. "Isn't that Tyler Mack?"

"I think it is!" Bess leaned forward to get a better view. "Yep. I recognize the red hair."

As the escalator descended, Nancy realized that Tyler was shopping at a watch counter. She pulled Bess off the moving stairs when they reached the bottom and ushered her behind a group of mannequins in spring clothes. There they had a good view of Mack.

Tyler was pointing to a watch in the case, which the clerk handed to him reverently. "Wow! That's a gold watch, Nancy," Bess said, craning her neck to see.

Apparently, Tyler liked the look of the watch. He nodded to the clerk, who helped him fasten it on his wrist.

As Nancy and Bess watched, he pulled a thick wad of bills out of his pocket and peeled hundreds of dollars in cash from it.

"Look at all that cash!" Bess whispered. "He must be a millionaire!"

"Why would a millionaire work at the zoo?" Nancy murmured.

Still admiring his new watch, the assistant zookeeper headed for the exit. "Let's see where he goes," Nancy said to Bess. Keeping their distance, they followed him across the store.

Tyler never looked back, so the girls picked up speed until they were only a few yards behind him. When he left the store, he headed over to an expensive-looking red sports car. After pausing to rub a spot off the car's mirrorlike finish, he slid in and drove away.

"Should we follow him?" Bess asked.

"Might as well," Nancy said. It was easy to keep an eye on Tyler's conspicuous car. After a short ride, however, Tyler led them straight back to the zoo. He parked in the staff lot and hurried away.

"It must have been his lunch hour," Bess said.

Nancy shook her head. "It's too early for lunch, but I wonder where all that money came from?" she commented. "I doubt that he earns enough to buy such an expensive watch."

"Maybe Mr. Berry will tell you his salary," Bess suggested. "Meanwhile, I hate to be the one who always brings this up, but I'm starving. My stomach says it's lunchtime—no matter what the clock says. Why don't you come over and we'll have something to eat?"

Nancy nodded. "I'll pick up my car, and we can wait for George to call." She jogged over to her Mustang in the zoo parking lot. "See you soon," she said as Bess drove off with a wave.

Half an hour later Nancy and Bess were in Bess's kitchen making tuna melts. As soon as the girls put the sandwiches in the oven, the phone rang. "It's George," Bess mouthed to Nancy. She was quiet for a few minutes, then turned to Nancy. "George wants us to go with her and Owen to a movie tonight," she told Nancy. "A lot of people from the zoo will be there."

Nancy nodded. It was a good chance to keep an eye on Tyler. "What time?"

"Eight o'clock. It's a film about wildlife preservation, with a lecture afterward." Bess listened for another minute and turned to Nancy, holding her hand over the mouthpiece. "George says we can have our brainstorming session after the film. She and Owen are 'busy' this afternoon, if you get my drift." Bess raised her eyebrows as she told Nancy this piece of news.

"I guess it's okay," Nancy said with a rueful grin. "I'd hate to stand in the way of true love."

Bess confirmed the plans with George and hung up.

"I'm not nuts about the idea of a nature film," Bess admitted to Nancy. "But I guess it's important."

"Is the film at the zoo?" Nancy asked.

"No, it's at the River Heights Country Club. Apparently, it's been set up for a while—it's a benefit for the zoo." Suddenly Bess's face fell. "Oh, gosh, I just remembered. I can't go."

"Why not?" Nancy asked.

"I promised Ted I'd see him tonight."

Nancy shot her friend an impatient look. "Bess, can't you cancel? I'd really like your help on this one."

The look on Nancy's face must have made her friend think twice. "Okay," she said finally. "If it were true love, I wouldn't cancel. But Ted is only a true crush."

The country club was lit up outside with tiny white bulbs. It looked like fairyland. Inside, zoo employees and patrons milled around among masses of potted plants strung with more tiny lights and festooned with gold ribbons and bows.

"Look at those dresses," Bess said, with awe, after they hung up their coats. Although it wasn't strictly a formal affair, many of the women were wearing strapless dresses in jewel-like colors.

Nancy, Bess, and George had all chosen to wear two-piece outfits. Bess looked fetching in a drift of pink chiffon, while George was tailored in black and white checkerboard squares. Nancy wore a high-collared emerald green silk shirt and pants that looked vaguely Chinese. All eyes turned and followed the three girls as they entered the main ballroom.

There was a delay in showing the film because of problems with the projector. "The technician says it will be about fifteen minutes," Maurice Berry announced. "Refreshments will be served in the lounge while we wait."

"Good. This will give us a chance to check out the crowd," Nancy said to Bess.

"And the jewelry," Bess commented, her eyes wide. "Just look at that diamond necklace!" she said, grabbing Nancy's arm and pointing at a glittering cascade of teardrop-shaped jewels.

"Let's concentrate on people from the zoo," Nancy told her. "Is Tyler here?"

"I haven't seen him yet," Bess said, her eyes still glued to the necklace.

"He's behind that pillar, talking to Zoe," said

71

Owen from behind them. He pointed in the direction of the door. "She just came in," he added, slipping an arm around George's waist and pulling her aside.

The chic zookeeper was still wearing her coat. She and Tyler appeared to be arguing about something.

Nancy inched closer to the arguing couple, followed by Bess. But before they were near enough to hear anything, Zoe looked up and saw them.

Nancy thought she saw a look of annoyance cross Zoe's face, but the zookeeper recovered easily and acted extremely friendly.

"I didn't know you were interested in conservation," she said, smiling at them. "It's so great that you could come." She made no reference to the scene at the zoo that morning.

Zoe blinked suddenly. "Oh, they're flashing the lights. That means it's time to go in."

She took Nancy's and Bess's arms, leaving Tyler standing alone. "Mind if I join you?" she asked. "We'll talk later, Tyler," she called back over her shoulder. He stared after her, an expression of fury crossing his face.

At the door to the theater Zoe left them. "I'm sure you'll want to find your friends, and so do I," she said excusing herself. "Enjoy the film!"

"What was that about?" Bess wondered as they looked around for George and Owen.

"I'm not sure. She's hard to figure out," Nancy

replied. The zookeeper had positively dripped friendliness.

"But so elegant! That little hat with the feather, and did you smell her perfume?" Bess enthused.

"I'm afraid I missed it," Nancy said. "Where are they?" she added, half to herself.

"They're probably sitting in the back somewhere, *alone,*" Bess said significantly. "Why don't we sit down and look for them afterward?"

Nancy agreed, and they found two seats near the front. Nancy found the movie fascinating—animal preservation was such a pressing issue. Among the endangered animals were several species of Asian civets. Although they had different markings from the civets at World of Africa, she could see a resemblance.

When the movie was over, Mr. Berry announced there would be a ten-minute break before the lecture. "Let's take a walk," Nancy suggested to Bess, standing up. Picking up their coats in the lobby, they ran into Owen and George. "Where were you two?" Bess asked.

"In the back," said George, reddening slightly. Bess raised her eyebrow at Nancy as if to say, "I told you so."

"We were on our way to get some fresh air," Bess continued. "Want to come?"

They all strolled down the walk leading to the parking lot. "It's nice here in the winter, isn't it?" George asked. "We usually only come in summer, to go swimming."

"Don't talk to me about swimming now." Bess shivered, pulling her cream-colored wool coat more tightly around her.

They reached the parking lot. "I guess we'd better go back," Nancy started to say when suddenly George grabbed her arm.

"Isn't that the car that tried to run you over?" she asked, pointing to a van that was backing out.

"I think so." Nancy strained her eyes, unable to make out the color of the van in the dark. "I'm going to check."

"I'm coming with you," George said firmly. They moved across the lot to investigate, being careful to stay in the shadows. Owen and Bess followed.

As they approached, the van finished pulling out and drove away at top speed. Once she got a closer look, Nancy was convinced it was the same one.

"At least the driver didn't notice us this time," George commented.

"He's going too fast for us to follow him," Nancy said disappointedly. "We'd never catch up."

"If it *was* a he," George pointed out. "I didn't see who was driving, did you?"

"No." Nancy frowned. She'd been so busy watching the van, she hadn't thought to check the identity of the driver.

"For what it's worth, I bet we'll see the van

again soon," George said, comforting her friend. "It keeps turning up."

"I guess so." Nancy turned away. "We might as well— What's that?"

"What?"

"I heard a noise." She held up her hand for quiet. "Listen, there it is again."

There was a faint scrabbling sound, followed by a thumping noise. "It's coming from over there," Nancy said, pointing to a nearby car.

"That's Owen's car!" George exclaimed. "The beat-up white one. Be careful," she added as Nancy ran over.

The noise was definitely coming from inside the car. Nancy tried the front door and found it unlocked.

She pulled the door open, and a bloodcurdling howl filled the air. Nancy smelled a strong, musky odor and saw fangs gleaming eerily in the darkness. Then she felt sharp claws rake her hand.

She was being attacked by a frenzied civet!

Chapter

Nine

HER HEART JUMPING, Nancy slammed the car door shut, trapping the civet inside. As it howled its frustration, George dashed to Nancy's side.

"What was that?" George's voice was high and reedy.

"A civet, I think," Nancy replied, speaking with a calm she didn't feel. They heard a thump as the civet threw itself against the car door, desperately trying to get out.

Nancy leaned against the door, feeling slightly faint. "I think it scratched me, but I'm all right."

"*All right!* Nancy, that's the second time you've almost been killed!" George was pale.

"When I saw that thing coming at you, I nearly died!"

Owen and Bess ran up to them. "I thought I heard a civet, but——" Owen stopped when he saw the gash on Nancy's hand. "Nancy, what happened?"

Bess let out a little scream. "You're bleeding! We've got to get you to the hospital right away!"

Nancy shook her head. "It's not that bad," she told them, taking a deep breath of the cold night air. The scratches on her hand throbbed a bit but weren't too painful.

Nancy turned to Owen. "There's a civet in your car—it looks pretty frightened."

Owen nodded. "I have some animal tranquilizers. But I think we should take care of that scratch first. I have a first-aid kit in my trunk," he told George, throwing her the keys.

While George unlocked the trunk and got out the kit, Owen examined Nancy's hand. "It's not too deep," he commented. George gave him the first-aid kit, and he swabbed the scratch with disinfectant. Then he applied a soothing ointment.

"That feels much better, thank you," Nancy said as Owen wrapped the scratch in a professional-looking bandage. "You should have been a doctor," she added.

"That's what my parents say, too," he said, smiling. Then his face grew serious. "Now I'd better take care of the civet."

"What is it doing here?" Bess wondered.

"Obviously, whoever was driving the van planted it," George said grimly.

The civet in the car gave a mournful howl. "I think we ought to deal with the poor animal before we talk about this," Nancy said. "The poor thing looks and sounds terrified."

Bess said, "Nancy, you sound like you feel sorry for it! After what it did to you . . ."

"But, Bess, it wasn't planning to hurt Nancy," Owen told her. "It acted out of instinct." He looked at the civet through the window. "Nancy's right, the civet is scared to death. That's why it's giving off that musky smell."

"Is that what civet oil smells like? It's awful," Bess said. "I can't believe it's used in perfumes!"

"They must neutralize it first," Nancy told her.

Owen gave Nancy and Bess a curious look. "How did you know about civet oil?" he asked.

Nancy explained what Felicity Willert had told her and Bess earlier that day. George let out a long, low whistle. "So that's what this is all about," she said.

"Maybe," Nancy said. "Except that it doesn't seem that civet oil is too hard to find. It's just expensive."

"And hard to cultivate," Owen added, taking a large canvas bag stamped River Heights Zoo from the trunk of the car. "You have to scrape their glands to retrieve the musk. Unless you know what you're doing, it's an impossible job."

Nancy listened carefully as she watched Owen take out a pair of leather gloves from the trunk. Next, he picked up a gun and loaded it with a long silver dart.

"It's a tranquilizer dart," he explained when Bess looked at him questioningly.

Motioning to the girls to stand back, Owen put on the leather gloves and opened the car door just a crack. The civet hissed at him. "Come on, girl," he said softly. "This will only hurt for a minute."

As the others watched, he managed to shoot a dart into the big cat's flank. He waited a minute, then opened the car door. "It's safe now," he assured them. "She'll be out for at least an hour."

The civet was collapsed on the front seat, breathing slowly. "Is it a female?" Nancy asked, noting his use of the word *she*.

Owen nodded. "It's the same civet that disappeared last night," he said grimly, examining the animal through the car window. "She's got a notched ear from a fight she was in a couple of months ago."

"What should we do now?" George asked. "You can't just take the civet home with you."

"I think the best thing would be to return her to the zoo," Owen said. "I have only one dart, so I don't want to risk having her wake up," he added.

"We'll come along," Nancy offered.

Owen nodded. "You'd better take George in your car," he said. "Mine smells pretty raunchy."

The girls piled into Nancy's Mustang, discussing who might have planted the civet. "It had to be the man with the sunglasses," George said. "Who else could have been driving that van?"

"But who is he out to get, Owen or Nancy?" Bess wondered.

"Maybe he thought we all came in one car," George suggested.

"Or maybe he's out to get all of us." Bess shuddered. "This is starting to feel very scary."

Nancy was only half listening to the conversation. Another thought had occurred to her—one she thought she'd better keep to herself for the time being. Why did Owen just happen to have leather gloves and a tranquilizer gun in the trunk of his car?

The equipment clearly belonged to the zoo—and Owen no longer worked at World of Africa. Maybe he had forgotten to return it, Nancy told herself. But why would he have been carrying a tranquilizer gun in the first place?

The questions nagged at her. She was sure Owen would never do anything to hurt the civets. But what if he thought they weren't being treated well enough at the zoo? Or what if he had some special experiment that he wanted to do privately?

Bess's voice penetrated her thoughts. "Earth to Nancy. Come in, Nancy," she was saying.

"Huh?"

"You looked like you were on another planet,"

Bess said. "I asked you three times why you thought someone else might have been driving the van."

"No real reason," she replied. "Still, since we didn't see the driver, I don't want to jump to conclusions. The man could be working with someone else."

Bess nodded, satisfied, and Nancy let her thoughts wander again. Why did she keep wondering about Owen? She hated feeling suspicious about her friend's boyfriend. Especially when George was so incredibly happy.

"Nancy!" George shouted in her ear. "Turn left!"

Quickly she turned and steered onto the street leading to the zoo. "You almost missed the turnoff," George said. "Are you all right?"

"Maybe she's still a little dazed from what happened," Bess suggested. "I would be."

"No, I'm fine," Nancy told them. Just then she slammed her foot on the brake, so hard that the three of them lurched forward.

"Now what is it?" Bess gazed worriedly at her friend.

"Nothing. There's a chain in front of the entrance to the parking lot, that's all." She pointed to the front of the car. Sure enough, the Mustang's headlights shone brightly on a thick chain stretched across the road.

"Thank goodness. For a minute there I thought you were cracking up," Bess said.

"I *was* daydreaming," Nancy told her. "But I'm fine now."

Owen drove up next to them. "What's wrong?" he asked, rolling down his window.

"Chain across the road," Nancy shouted back.

He got out to investigate, then came back to their car. "You need a key to open it. We'd better walk from here."

"Will you be able to carry the civet?" Nancy asked.

Owen nodded. "She's not that heavy."

Nancy backed up and parked her car off the road, in the shadow of some trees. Owen followed. Then they climbed over the chain and started walking across the parking lot to the zoo.

"This is really creepy," Bess whispered. The lot was deserted, and each footstep echoed twice against the buildings. On Owen's shoulder the civet stirred and mewed.

"Is she waking up?" Bess asked in a frightened voice.

Owen shook his head. "She's probably having a dream. Animals dream just like we do," he told her.

"As long as she's still sleeping," Bess said, glancing nervously at the civet.

Finally the group got to the gate of the zoo, only to find it locked and the security guard's booth empty.

"That's strange. I wonder where the guard is?" Owen commented.

"How will we get in?" George asked.

Owen checked his pockets. "No problem. I've still got my keys," he told her, fishing them out. "I forgot to return them to Zoe," he explained.

He led them to a small door in the gate and slipped the key into the lock. It opened silently, and the door swung back.

The three girls followed Owen inside. "The zoo is even scarier than the parking lot," Bess whispered nervously.

Nancy agreed. In the black night animals sighed or snored or groaned, but it was impossible to see them.

"There isn't even a moon," Bess noted.

They heard a loud squeal, followed by a splashing noise. Bess gave a little shriek. "What—what was that?" she cried.

"Probably a sea lion," Owen assured her. "They're in a tank right near here."

World of Africa was close to the zoo's main gate. They tiptoed around to the staff entrance, waited while Owen opened the door with his key, and slipped inside.

Inside it was dark and deserted. Not wanting to attract attention, Owen turned on only a small light near the door. "At least we'll be able to see where we're going," he explained. The others followed him down the long hallway to the door marked Civets.

"Whew, we made it!" Owen said to George as he opened the door. He sounded relieved. They entered the supply room, and he opened the door to the exhibit. Nancy, Bess, and George watched as he gently placed the sleeping civet inside.

As Owen was straightening up, the exhibit was suddenly awash with bright light.

Then a voice shouted out, "Nobody move. You're all under arrest!"

Chapter

Ten

NANCY SHIELDED HER EYES against the blinding light while Owen stood frozen in the doorway to the exhibit.

George pulled on Nancy's arm. "What is going on?"

"I don't know," Nancy said, "but I'm going to find out." She pushed past Owen and stood just inside the civet exhibit, keeping a close watch on the animals. Owen and George followed her, while Bess stayed in the supply room, looking scared and confused.

"Don't try anything!" the same man called out. "We've got you covered!"

Squinting, Nancy could see two figures approaching on the other side of the glass. They were running through the visitors' part of the exhibit. As her eyes adjusted, she recognized Harper Anderson, the zoo security guard. With him was another guard she didn't recognize.

"Just hold it right there while Joseph here comes around to get you," Harper shouted at them through the glass. "And I'd advise you not to put up a fight."

"Of course we won't." Owen had been silent, but now he exploded angrily. "We're not criminals, for pete's sake."

"Oh, no?" Harper returned. "Then what are you doing here?"

"We're returning a civet!" George cried.

"Tell that to the police," said Harper, obviously unconvinced. Two other people had come up behind him. Nancy made out the features of Zoe Spelios and Maurice Berry.

With a sinking feeling Nancy looked around her. She, Owen, George, and Bess had sneaked into World of Africa in the middle of the night. Owen was carrying a tranquilizer gun. Nancy had civet scratches on her hand. All the evidence added up. It looked as if they were stealing a civet, not returning one!

"Let go of me, you creep," Bess said. Nancy turned and saw Joseph pulling Bess out into the hall.

Nancy followed Owen and George out of the

exhibit, through the supply room, and into the hallway. Joseph was standing there talking to Harper Anderson.

"You see, Maurice," Zoe told the zoo director sadly. "The caller was right. Owen and his friends are behind the thefts."

"Wait just one minute!" Owen shouted. He was about to go on when George shot him a warning look. Owen must have realized that now wasn't the time for him to lose his temper, because he closed his mouth and sullenly looked down at the floor.

Nancy wasn't going to give up so easily. "What caller?" she asked Zoe.

Zoe explained. "I received an anonymous phone call at the country club warning me that Owen and his friends were about to steal another civet, and that if I got to the zoo quickly I could catch them."

She sighed heavily. "I thought it was a crank call, but I couldn't just ignore it. When I told Maurice, he decided to come along."

Mr. Berry said angrily, "You kids really made fools of us, didn't you? Especially you, Nancy."

Bess jumped to their defense. "We haven't done anything," she told him. "We were returning a civet, not taking one!"

"Returning it from where?" Berry asked scornfully. "Did you find it on the street?"

Nancy tried to reason with the zoo director. "Of course not. We—"

He motioned for her to be quiet. "I don't want to hear it. I trusted you and gave you the run of the zoo. And this is how you repay my trust." He shook his head, disgusted. "I'm turning this whole thing over to the police."

"I'm afraid I have to agree with you," Zoe said with resigned determination.

"Wait!" Bess said suddenly, surprising all of them. "Count them!"

"Count what?" asked Berry, confused. George looked at her friend as though she'd lost her mind.

But Nancy understood. "Count the civets!" she said. "After the last theft, there were only five. Now there should be six." She smiled at her friend. Good old Bess! Leave it to her to come through in a crisis!

"The civets have been disturbed too much already," Zoe said angrily. "I think this should wait until tomorrow."

"It will take only a minute," Owen pointed out.

"From a security standpoint, I'd rather get this resolved right away," added Harper.

"Then let's go," Owen said, leading the way to the visitors' entrance to the exhibit. "We'll be able to count them more easily this way," he explained.

The lights were still on in the exhibit when Owen stepped up to the glass with Nancy,

George, and Bess at his heels. Zoe, Maurice, Harper, and Joseph followed reluctantly. Nancy could tell they thought this was crazy.

Three civets were immediately visible: the drugged one, who was just beginning to wake up, and two others, who were sniffing around her.

"That's three," Harper said. At that moment a fourth civet came out from behind a bush and joined the others.

"That's the fourth," Owen said. "And there's a fifth one asleep on that branch." He pointed to a tree in one corner with a civet crouching near the top.

"And the sixth?" Mr. Berry asked.

Owen looked around. "I don't see it," he admitted finally. "It must be hiding."

"Or missing," Zoe said.

"Look!" Nancy cried. "Didn't something move over by the water bowl?"

The others leaned forward. "I don't see— Wait, there *is* something," Mr. Berry said.

"There it is!" Bess cried as the sixth civet crawled out from under a stand of shrubbery.

Nancy breathed a huge sigh of relief. "You see, we aren't thieves," she told Mr. Berry.

To her surprise the zoo director was still angry. "That doesn't explain what you were all doing here in the middle of the night—after you were forbidden to come at all," he added to Owen. "And one of those civets looks sick."

"We had to drug it," Owen explained.

Berry frowned. "There's another thing I don't understand," he said. "How did you get in here?"

Zoe shot Owen a questioning look. "That's precisely what I wanted to know."

"I still have my keys," Owen admitted quietly.

"Give them to me," Berry said. While Owen was fumbling with his keychain, Berry said to Zoe, "I'm going to authorize a full-scale investigation into this case. I should have done it long ago, but you told me you could handle it."

The zookeeper's eyes narrowed. Nancy thought she was about to say something scathing, but instead, Zoe just nodded silently.

"In the meantime," he said to the others, "I don't want to see you on the grounds for any reason. You're forbidden to enter the zoo, do you understand?" He glared at them. "Now, get out. Now."

Nancy could tell the zoo director meant business. "Come on, guys," she said. "Let's go."

George nodded. Under Berry's watchful eye the four of them filed from the exhibit room and walked out to the parking lot in silence.

"I don't think he believed us," Bess said with a sigh.

"Me, neither," Nancy confirmed. "We really need to talk this through. Let's all go to my house."

"I'll ride with Owen," George said. They

hopped into his beat-up car, while Nancy and Bess got into her Mustang.

The two friends were silent on the drive to Nancy's house, still somewhat stunned by Berry's ultimatum. As she pulled up to her house and shut off the ignition, Nancy said, "Not being able to go back to the zoo is going to put a serious damper on this investigation."

Bess nodded and got out of the car. Owen and George pulled up behind Nancy.

"So much for good deeds," George said, coming up to them.

"Yeah, what a bust," Bess agreed, staring at the ground.

"Let's go inside and have some hot chocolate," Nancy said, leading the way to the Drews' front door. "The four of us should be able to come up with a plan."

Within a few minutes the four were seated around the Drews' kitchen table with steaming cups of hot chocolate in front of them.

"One thing's for sure," Nancy said, warming her hands on her mug. "Someone put the civet in Owen's car on the assumption he'd bring it back to the zoo. Then that same someone called Zoe."

Owen nodded silently and pursed his lips in thought.

"Setup city," George agreed. "But who?"

"That's obvious," Bess said. "The man with the sunglasses."

"We still don't know that," Nancy cautioned her. "We didn't see the van driver. We're not even sure that the person who was driving the van put the civet in the car."

"But who would want to do such a thing?" George asked.

"I can think of at least one person," Nancy told her. "Tyler Mack."

"But he was at the movie," Bess said.

"We're not sure about that. We only saw him outside the theater. He could have planted the civet in the car, then called Zoe to set Owen up."

"Why?" Owen wondered. "If Tyler was trying to get rid of me, he's already succeeded. Why set me up for this, too?"

"Maybe he just hates you," Bess suggested.

"That's possible," Nancy agreed. "Or maybe he wants to throw suspicion off himself," she said thoughtfully. "There are some things about Tyler that don't add up."

"Like where does he get so much money?" Bess said. Seeing George and Owen's confused looks, Nancy quickly explained what they'd seen at Daly's.

"That's very weird," Owen said when she was finished. "He's always complaining to anyone who will listen about how little he makes."

"Well, somewhere along the way he got a raise," Bess said.

"I don't see how," Owen said. "Zoe doesn't

like him, either, and she's the one in charge of salaries."

Nancy thought about it. "Maybe he found another way to make extra cash," she said finally.

Bess asked, "But how?"

"I can think of one way," Owen said ominously, obviously catching Nancy's train of thought. "Selling stolen civets!"

Chapter

Eleven

"WE CAN'T JUMP THE GUN," Nancy said slowly. "Still, it's a very strong possibility." She laid out the facts. "One: Tyler Mack has access to the exhibit, and, two, he's got a suspiciously large amount of money at his disposal."

George gave a long whistle. "It does make sense. If only there was a way to keep an eye on him," she said. "But with none of us allowed in the zoo . . ."

"There may be a way for us to get back in," Owen began. He rubbed his chin thoughtfully.

"I don't know," George said. "Mr. Berry seemed pretty upset about the whole thing."

"George is right," Owen said. He leaned forward and rested his elbows on the table, then looked up knowingly at Nancy, Bess, and George. "There is one person who might help, though."

"Who?" Bess asked.

"Zoe," Owen answered.

"She's always liked you," George agreed.

"And she seemed pretty embarrassed about what's been going on," Nancy added, remembering Zoe's public humiliation. "She might like the idea of having us continue the investigation. It would help her save face," she pointed out.

Owen nodded silently, while George's face lit up. "I think it'll work, Nancy," she said. "Meanwhile, how about some more cocoa?"

Everyone nodded yes except Bess, who covered her cup with her hand. "None for me, thanks. All that sugar will make me blow up like a balloon."

At ten o'clock the next morning Nancy found herself outside Zoe Spelios's office. She had thought about calling Zoe ahead of time, but didn't want to risk being told by the zookeeper not to come. Instead, Nancy decided to take a chance that Zoe would be in.

"Can I help you?" A woman dressed in a business suit and high heels had come up to Nancy just as she was about to knock.

"Is Zoe Spelios here?" Nancy asked.

"I'll get her." The woman knocked on Zoe's office door. "Someone here to see you."

Zoe looked beyond the woman and noticed Nancy. The confused look on her face quickly disappeared. "Thanks, Robin. I'll see her," Zoe said. As Nancy went in, she explained, "I've fallen so behind on my paperwork that I had to get a temporary secretary."

Nancy noticed, once again, how chicly Zoe was dressed. She wore a tailored coatdress of red wool with large black buttons down the front, and matching black onyx earrings. The outfit seemed a little formal for her position at a zoo, but Zoe managed to pull it off.

"Now, what can I do for you?" Zoe asked, breaking in on Nancy's thoughts. "I assume you have a good reason for being here after what Maurice Berry told you last night. You could get in a lot of trouble if he knew you were here."

Nancy opened her mouth to answer, but Zoe went on. "Don't worry—I won't tell him."

Deciding to trust the zookeeper, Nancy dived into her story. "Actually, I was hoping we might be able to help each other. If you arrange with Mr. Berry for me to be allowed back on the zoo grounds, and I find the missing civets, that will help you, right?"

Zoe leaned back in her chair and gave Nancy a small smile. "So you want to reach an agreement, then? You're very smart for your age, Ms. Drew."

Nancy gave Zoe a thoughtful look. This all seemed like a game to the zookeeper. She took a deep breath and went on. "I was hoping we could include Owen, too. Let him continue with his work," she added. "It's very important to him."

Zoe nodded sympathetically. "He's a good researcher," she said. "Believe me, I'm sorry to lose him, but there's nothing I can do. Maurice is in charge of all the work-study students, and he's dead set against having Owen remain."

"But Mr. Berry must realize by now that we weren't stealing the civet. We were returning it," Nancy said. "Couldn't we ask him to reconsider Owen's case? When we explain what happened last night—"

Zoe cut her off. "It's very nice of you to come to Owen's defense, but I can tell you right now that Maurice won't listen."

The phone rang, and Zoe reached out to answer it. Her hand froze in midair as the secretary picked it up in the other room. "I'm not used to having someone take my phone calls," she said with a little laugh.

"I'm sorry, you have the wrong number. This isn't Classic Sense," Nancy heard the secretary say. The girl's voice grew more agitated. "Yes, I'm new here, but I know perfectly well what—"

Swiftly Zoe stood up and called out, "Is there something wrong, Robin?" She said to Nancy, "Excuse me, but I don't want her getting all upset her first day."

"Of course," Nancy agreed.

"I'll be back in a minute," Zoe said. "Make yourself at home."

After Zoe left, Nancy looked around the zookeeper's office. Except for the photographs and memorabilia she'd noticed the day before, everything was very businesslike. There were papers and files everywhere.

On a table by the desk Nancy spotted a thick, obviously expensive book with a fancy marble-paper cover. It looked so out of place among the papers that she went over for a closer look.

The book's title was *Fit for a Queen*. She was about to leaf through it when Zoe returned. Nancy quickly stood back from the table.

"Now, where were we?" the zookeeper asked brightly. She glanced at her watch. "Oh, dear, I can't really spare you any more time, Nancy."

Nancy started to protest, but Zoe just smiled and walked her to the door. "I'll tell you what," she said. "I'll talk to Maurice about Owen and get back to you. And maybe I can get you reinstated on the case," Zoe added. "You could help me by finding those missing civets."

"That would be great," said Nancy. Things were looking up. "Could I call you tomorrow?"

"Uh—why don't you give me a couple of days?" Zoe said. "I'm not sure when I'll be able to get to him," she explained.

Nancy had no choice but to agree. "Thanks again for your help," she said.

"No problem," Zoe said with a smile. "Now be sure to leave right away, and don't let anyone see you."

Nancy walked quickly out the way she had come, keeping her head down to avoid being noticed. She frowned as she ran over the meeting with Zoe in her mind. Nancy didn't really trust Zoe's promise of help. The zookeeper was friendly enough, but she didn't seem in a hurry to talk to Mr. Berry.

Zoe could just be giving me the brush-off, Nancy thought, slipping into her car. If she wanted results, she'd have to talk with Mr. Berry herself.

Nancy was about to get back out of her Mustang when she saw a sleek white sports car start to back out of its space. The driver turned sharply, then roared in Nancy's direction at what seemed like a hundred miles an hour.

As the car shot past her, Nancy glanced into the driver's seat, catching a glimpse of red wool. It was Zoe, and she was obviously in a big hurry.

Instantly abandoning her plan to see Mr. Berry, Nancy turned the key in the ignition and followed in the direction the white car had taken. Zoe drove like a maniac along the quiet back roads, running stop signs and taking turns at top speed. The roar of her engine, punctuated by squeals as she hit the brakes, broke the stillness of the winter morning.

Does she always drive like this? Nancy wondered, struggling to keep up, but maintaining her distance. Her Mustang handled like a dream, even on the twisting roads, but the sports car was powerful, and Zoe had a big lead, which she managed to keep.

After several minutes of winding roads, Nancy followed Zoe into a more residential section of town. There the zookeeper had to slow down a bit. Nancy made up some of the distance between them, being careful to stay out of Zoe's sight.

Then, abruptly, Zoe swung her car into a shopping center and screeched to a stop in front of a drugstore. Just my luck, Nancy thought, pulling up a short distance away. She takes me on a breakneck chase, and she's just going to get some cough drops.

But what Nancy saw next made her sit up and take notice. A man came out of the drugstore, hurried over to Zoe's car, and leaned into the now-open passenger window. His face was turned so Nancy couldn't see it.

As Nancy watched, the man took what looked like a gun out of a bag he was carrying and waved it at the zookeeper. Nancy gasped. Was the man threatening Zoe at gunpoint?

Instead of acting afraid, Zoe stuck her hand out the window and took the gun from the man.

The two talked for a while in what looked like an intimate way. Nancy quelled her curiosity.

There was no way for her to get closer without being seen by Zoe and the mystery man.

Finally the man handed Zoe the bag, along with another object that Nancy couldn't make out.

Waving goodbye, Zoe drove away in a cloud of exhaust. The man remained where he was and watched her go.

Slowly Nancy inched her car forward until she could see the man's face.

It was Owen!

Chapter

Twelve

OWEN WAS LOOKING around nervously, so Nancy ducked her head below the windshield.

Satisfied that no one had noticed his conversation with Zoe, the blond college student walked to his car and drove away. Nancy drove after him, her mind spinning.

Why had Owen given Zoe that gun? Obviously it was the same tranquilizer gun he'd used on the civet the night before. Had Zoe lent it to him, and was he returning it? If so, why?

Nancy flashed back to her conversation with Owen the night before. He had been pretty sure the zookeeper would be sympathetic to his case, she remembered.

Still thinking, Nancy followed Owen's car through the center of town. There were two possibilities, she thought, neither of them very attractive. Zoe and Owen could be working together to steal the civets. That didn't explain why Zoe would bring Mr. Berry down to "catch" Owen and the rest of them, though. Unless she was trying a double-cross.

The second possibility was that Zoe and Owen were secretly involved. Maybe the college student was infatuated with his elegant boss, Nancy thought unhappily. Zoe could be the mastermind behind the thefts, with Owen doing her bidding.

He might have a big enough crush on her to do anything she asked, even letting her set him up for the thefts. Zoe could have told him that she'd protect him, and that the thefts were somehow necessary to the civets' well-being.

Nancy shook her head, realizing that her thoughts were going off in wild directions. There was no proof of a connection between Zoe and Owen, just one meeting that Nancy happened to witness. Still, she couldn't discount the possibility.

Nancy followed Owen's car around a corner and onto a familiar road. He was going to George's house, Nancy realized. Poor George! If Owen had something going with Zoe, it would break her friend's heart.

Nancy watched as Owen's car pulled up to George's door. The blond boy got out, ran up the walk, and pressed the bell. As the door opened, Nancy drove off. She didn't want George to see her.

Nancy drove home slowly, not sure what to do next. Was Owen capable of leading George on? She just didn't know. As Nancy let herself into the empty house, she was feeling frustrated and confused. Absently she hung up her jacket, then noticed the message light blinking on the answering machine.

She rewound the machine and played the messages back. Two people had called for her father. She wrote down their names and numbers, noting the time of the calls.

Then, just as she was about to turn the machine off, the deep voice of Ned Nickerson filled the room.

"Hey, Drew, it's been a while since I've heard from you!" the recording said. "Hope you've been thinking about me, even if you can't find time to call." Then her boyfriend's voice grew softer. "Seriously, I wanted to find out how everything's going. Don't forget, I'm here if you need me."

The message clicked off. Nancy tried calling Ned back, but his roommate said he'd gone to class. "Tell him I got his message just when I needed it most," she said. She hung up, after promising to call again later.

Nancy smiled to herself—Ned was so sweet.

Sometimes when things got rough, she *did* forget he was there, but he always managed to remind her.

She stood thoughtfully by the phone for another minute, then dialed Bess's number. She needed to talk to someone about Owen—and when it came to boys, Bess was the expert.

Bess answered the phone. "Hello?"

"Hi, it's Nancy. Can I come over? I need to talk."

Her friend's voice warmed up. "I'm here."

"I'll be over in ten minutes," Nancy said. As she hung up the receiver, she chided herself for letting the case get her down. She'd solve it yet—with a little help from her friends.

"That jerk! That unbelievable heel!" Bess was nearly shrieking. Nancy had just filled her in on Owen's meeting with Zoe. "How could he do this to George?"

Nancy tried to calm her down. "We don't know for sure that he's done anything," she pointed out.

"I knew there was something wrong the minute I met him," Bess continued, ignoring her. "He's too slick and sure of himself." She impatiently tapped her fingers on the table. "Boy, am I going to give him a piece of my mind!"

"So you think he could have a crush on Zoe?" Nancy asked.

"Think it? I'm practically positive!" Bess cried. "What are we going to do about it?" she demanded.

"I don't think we should do anything yet," Nancy said, not feeling as sure as Bess that Owen did like Zoe. "We don't have any proof."

"You saw them together!"

"It could have been anything," Nancy said. "Zoo business, or a coincidence—although it definitely didn't look like a coincidence," she admitted.

"This is going to kill George, just kill her," Bess said bitterly. "I don't think she's ever fallen so hard for a guy before."

"Bess, I really don't think we should tell her yet," Nancy said firmly. "She's going to be really upset, so what's the point?" She leaned forward. "There are still a lot of pieces missing."

"Like what?" Bess asked. "Zoe is stealing the civets, and Owen's so crazy about her that he's helping."

"Maybe. But what about Tyler Mack? He's obviously involved somehow. And what about the guy with the sunglasses?"

"What about them?" Bess asked. "No matter where they fit in, Owen is still a skunk. And we've got to tell George about it before she gets even more involved."

Nancy sighed. "There's another thing to consider." She spoke slowly, choosing her words carefully. "If we tell George, she'll probably want to confront Owen. If he is involved and she talks to him, it could wreck the whole investigation."

"So we'll ask her to wait," Bess said. "What's the big deal?"

"I just don't think we should risk it," Nancy said. "I think we should wait and see if we find definite proof."

Bess was silent for a minute, tapping the tabletop. When she spoke again, her voice was hard with determination. "I'm going to tell her about it. I'm sorry, Nancy, but George's feelings are a lot more important to me than an investigation."

"They're important to me, too. Don't you see, that's why I think we should wait," Nancy pleaded. Bess was already putting on her coat.

"I'm going to George's house right now," she said. "Are you coming or not?"

Nancy nodded. "I'll ride over with you."

Bess was tight-lipped, obviously still furious. She stared straight ahead as she drove, refusing even to glance at Nancy.

Nancy's thoughts were in a whirl. Was her desire to get to the bottom of the case really more important than George's feelings?

"Pull up slowly," Nancy cautioned Bess as they approached George's block. "Owen may still be there."

Bess said grimly, "I hope he is. I've got a few things to say to him." When they got to George's house, Owen's car was gone.

Bess parked and bounded up the walk, followed by a reluctant Nancy. George answered the door almost the minute they rang the bell.

"Back so soon? Oh, it's you," George said. "I thought you were Owen. He was just here and forgot his scarf." She held up a red-and-gray wool muffler. "I thought he was coming back for it."

Bess looked at the muffler in disgust. "Get that away from me," she said. "I don't want anything to do with him."

"With Owen?" George looked baffled. "What are you talking about?"

Without hesitating, Bess went inside and spilled out the whole story, including their suspicions that Zoe and Owen were romantically involved. When she got to that part, George flinched and looked as if she'd been hit in the stomach.

When Bess had run out of steam, there was a long silence. Then Nancy started to say, "I'm really sorry—"

George interrupted her. "Bess, how do you know all this?" she asked. "About Owen and Zoe supposedly seeing each other?"

"Nancy was following Zoe," Bess explained. "She saw them meet in front of Kirkland's Drugstore."

"So this whole thing was your idea?" George asked, turning to Nancy.

"I don't have any proof," she answered honestly. "I was worried when I saw Owen and Zoe talking, so I told Bess about it."

"That's not all you did, is it?" George asked her. "You also followed Owen to my house earlier. I thought I saw your car, but when you didn't come in, I figured it must have been someone else."

Nancy nodded, reddening, as Bess looked at her in surprise. "You didn't tell me you followed him," she said.

Before Nancy could answer, George cut in. "You were spying on us, weren't you?" she said angrily. "You know, Nancy, your detective work is a lot more important to you than your friends."

"How can you say that?" Nancy asked, upset by her friend's accusations. She'd only taken on this case because of George!

"Because it's true!" George shouted at her. "You don't care about me. The only thing that matters to you is the case." She spat out the words as if they were choking her. "I've had it with you and your suspicions. And I've had it with being your friend!"

Chapter

Thirteen

GEORGE RAN OUT of the room as Nancy remained standing, stunned. She had never imagined that George could react so bitterly.

Bess touched her arm. "Wow. Sorry about that," she said awkwardly. "I thought she'd be mad at Owen, not you."

"Maybe I should go talk to her," Nancy said quietly.

"You'd better wait awhile," Bess said. "Give her time to cool off."

"I guess so." George's accusations really hurt. Nancy didn't think her work was more important to her than her friendships. Sometimes in the course of her detective work, things became dangerous, and protecting her friends was more important than sparing their feelings.

As though reading her mind, Bess said, "I'm sure George knows we didn't mean to hurt her. She's just upset about Owen." She sat down and buried her head in her hands. "You were right. I should have kept my big mouth shut."

"Well, there's nothing we can do about it now," Nancy said.

Suddenly they heard a loud, whirring noise from upstairs.

"That's George's stationary bicycle," Bess said as Nancy looked up, puzzled. "She takes out all her frustrations on it."

"It sounds like she's going a hundred miles an hour," Nancy said.

"Good! Exercise is the best medicine," said Bess briskly. "It'll distract her. And speaking of distraction," she added brightly, "I think you need one, too. How about lunch and maybe a little shopping?"

Nancy shook her head, smiling. She appreciated her friend's attempts to cheer her up, but she knew she couldn't rest yet. The quickest way to win George's friendship back was to solve the mystery.

"Could you drop me off at Daly's?" she asked Bess. "I want to ask Ms. Willert a few more questions about civet oil. As far as I'm concerned, that's the key to why the civets have been disappearing."

Bess nodded knowingly. "It's got to be, and she'd be the one to know." Nancy's friend looked up at the ceiling where the sound of George working out on her bicycle could still be heard. "I just hope we get to the bottom of this soon, Nancy."

"Me, too, Bess. Me, too."

"Nancy, Bess, how nice!" Felicity Willert smiled and stood up from behind her desk.

Before Nancy could say anything, Bess cried, "Oh, I love your outfit!" The perfume buyer was wearing a white silk jacket over a soft, plum-colored wool dress. The effect was simple yet very elegant.

"It's Italian, isn't it?" Nancy asked.

Ms. Willert nodded. "You have a good eye. It's by Gianni Moscatelli, the designer."

"It's beautiful," Bess said.

"I wanted to ask a few more questions about perfume making," Nancy explained.

Ms. Willert nodded. "What would you like to know?"

"Is civet oil expensive enough that someone would want their own personal supply of civets?" Nancy asked, searching for a motive for stealing the civets.

Felicity Willert looked confused. "It costs quite a lot, since civets are rare animals. But it would be impossible to have your own supply of civets. That has to be illegal."

"I'm sure it is," Bess said.

"Actually," the perfume buyer went on, "it's such a coincidence you should be interested in this whole issue. After I talked to you the other day, I got a phone call about a very rare perfume called Belle Soirée. It's been off the market for ten years, but it was one of the most famous perfumes made with civet oil."

"Belle Soirée?" Nancy repeated. "Do you have a sample?"

"Unfortunately, no." Felicity Willert took an ornate book off a shelf behind her desk. "But this history of perfume will tell you everything you need to know about it."

Nancy examined the ornate book the buyer held out to her. As she looked at it, a thrill went through her. *Fit for a Queen!* It was the same book Zoe Spelios kept in her office!

Nancy's mind started to race. If the zookeeper was interested in perfume and had access to civets . . .

Ms. Willert interrupted her thoughts. *"Fit for a Queen* is an important reference work on the history of perfume," she explained.

Eagerly Nancy leafed through the book. She arrived at the page describing Belle Soirée and quickly scanned the page. "It says here that the formula for Belle Soirée was lost when the man who developed the perfume sold his company."

"That explains why the perfume is so valuable," Bess said, leaning over Nancy's shoulder to read from the book.

"Exactly," Felicity Willert said.

Next to the description of the perfume was an old-fashioned black-and-white photograph showing a tall, thin man in a black suit. He was staring straight at the camera with a challenging look on his face.

The photo's caption read, "Jacques Mathieu, creator of Belle Soirée." Nancy stared intently at it.

"When did you say the creator of Belle Soirée died?" she asked Ms. Willert.

"About ten years ago," she replied.

Nancy looked up, baffled. "Are you sure?"

"Of course," the buyer told her, frowning slightly. "It was an important event in the perfume industry."

"I'm sorry, I didn't mean to doubt you," Nancy told her. "It's just that I'm positive I've seen this face before."

Bess, who had been studying the picture over her shoulder, looked at Nancy in surprise. "That's funny, I was just thinking the same thing!" she commented.

Ms. Willert shook her head. "I don't see how that's possible. Maybe you saw someone who resembled Jacques Mathieu."

"Maybe," Nancy said, not wanting to seem rude. Still, the longer she stared at the photograph, the surer she became that she'd seen him somewhere before.

She sat, lost in thought, until Bess nudged her. "You probably need to get back to work," Bess was saying to Ms. Willert. "Thanks very much for your help."

"Yes, thank you," Nancy echoed, jumping to her feet.

Ms. Willert smiled. "My pleasure. Come back anytime."

Bess led the way out of her office and down the escalator. "You know, that Jacques Mathieu looked really familiar," she told Nancy again as they went down the escalator.

Nancy nodded thoughtfully. The photograph was very old-fashioned—where had she seen one like it recently?

Suddenly Nancy grabbed Bess's arm. "I've got it!" she cried. "At least, I think I do."

"Got what?" Bess asked.

"Where I've seen a photo of Jacques Mathieu. I need to find a telephone," Nancy continued.

"There's a bank of them by the front door," Bess told her. Nancy jumped the last few steps of the escalator and went running for a pay phone, with Bess in hot pursuit.

Swiftly Nancy called information. "Do you have a number for Classic Sense?" she asked.

The operator gave her one. "How about an address?" Nancy asked. She wrote it down: 449 Bridgewater Road. "Could you tell me how that's spelled?" She paused. "No, not the street, the company. Thank you."

"What's Classic Sense?" Bess asked as Nancy got off the phone.

Nancy explained the conversation she'd overheard in Zoe's office earlier that day. "I thought it was *S-e-n-s-e*, but it's *S-c-e-n-t-s.*"

"Classic Scents! A perfume company?" Bess guessed. "What does Zoe Spelios have to do with a perfume company?"

"A lot, I'm starting to think," Nancy told her. "She keeps a copy of that photograph of Jacques Mathieu in her office, along with a copy of that history of perfume. I just realized that that was where I'd seen the picture before!"

She tapped the address in front of her. "Forget lunch, Bess, we're headed for Four forty-nine Bridgewater Road."

"But that's in the factory section," Bess protested. "I can't believe a glamorous perfume company would have offices there."

"Maybe it's a perfume factory, not an office," Nancy said. "Either way, we're going to find out," she added. "Let's go!"

As Bess drove, Nancy summed up what they knew so far. "First, Zoe has something to do with a company called Classic Scents. It's probably a perfume company, but we're not sure."

She continued. "Second, Zoe also has some connection with Jacques Mathieu, who created

Belle Soirée—a perfume that's made with civet musk."

"And Zoe works with civets," Bess put in excitedly.

"*And* the civets keep disappearing," Nancy reminded her. Her pulse raced, as it always did when she was getting close to the heart of a mystery.

Bess turned the car onto Bridgewater Road. "Some neighborhood, huh?" she commented. The street was full of potholes and lined with warehouses and abandoned buildings.

"There's one thing about all this I don't get," Bess continued. "That picture we saw of Jacques Mathieu looked familiar to me, too, but I'd never seen the photograph in Zoe's office."

"Maybe it's in other reference books," Nancy suggested. "Didn't you read a bunch of them when you were doing research for the party?"

"That could be it—I guess," Bess said, thinking, but she didn't sound convinced.

They reached number 449, an old warehouse with boarded-up windows. "This doesn't look like much of anything, let alone a perfume company," Bess commented as they parked.

Nancy led the way to the door of the building. She looked for a bell, but couldn't find one. Instead she knocked several times. No one answered.

"I think I hear something or someone moving around inside," Bess whispered nervously. Nancy put her ear to the door. Sure enough, something was moving around.

She knocked again, harder this time. Just then she noticed a strong, musky odor in the air. "Do you smell something?" she asked Bess.

Bess sniffed, and the two girls exchanged glances. "Civets!" Nancy said.

From behind them a heavily accented voice barked, "Put your hands up!"

Startled, Nancy spun around—to find herself staring straight into the barrel of a pistol!

Chapter

Fourteen

BESS TURNED AROUND and gasped. "Not you!" she said slowly.

A small sneer caught the side of the dark-haired man's mouth. But behind the mirrored sunglasses it was impossible for Nancy to read the man's full expression.

"Did you hear me? Hands up!" the man commanded them. "You two are much too nosy," he said ominously. He pointed with the gun to the door. "Inside."

As Nancy turned the knob, the musky smell grew stronger. What would they find inside? She whispered to Bess, "Get ready to run. The civets might be loose."

Bess didn't seem to hear her. She was staring at the man in sunglasses as if she'd seen a ghost.

"What is it?" Nancy asked, nudging her friend. "What's wrong?"

Bess's voice shook as she whispered, "Don't you recognize him? It's Jacques Mathieu!"

Nancy gasped. Bess was right—their captor bore an uncanny resemblance to the man in the photograph!

With an impatient wave of his pistol, the man motioned them inside. Her heart in her throat, Nancy pushed the door to the warehouse open.

Inside it was dark except for a few rays of light filtering in around a boarded-up window. One of the narrow shafts of light fell on a fenced-off area in a far corner of the room.

Nancy breathed a sigh of relief. The civets were penned up, not free. Then she felt Bess clutching her arm.

"Is—is it him?" Bess whispered, shivering from the cold and, Nancy suspected, from fright.

"Of course not—he's much too young," she said, trying to reassure her friend, who was obviously terrified. "Although there's definitely a resemblance."

Meanwhile, the man had been groping for something with his free hand. He kept the gun trained on them at all times. Now he was holding up a length of rope.

"I regret that I will have to leave you here," he

said. "It is very cold, but at least you will have the satisfaction of being with your little furry friends." He waved his hand at the civets. "Filthy animals, no?" he asked, looking at them with disgust. "That smell, *mon dieu!* But even their fear serves its purpose."

"To make oil for your perfumes?" Nancy asked, hoping to draw him out.

"How clever you are," he said with a sneer. "You have wasted a lot of our time, you and your friends."

"Why don't you just buy civet oil from suppliers?" Nancy asked, fishing for information.

"Be quiet," the man snapped at her, "or I will leave you inside the pen with the civets, not outside it." He threw something into the pen, causing one of the civets to give a frightened yelp and release more of the odorous musk.

Nancy's teeth were beginning to chatter from the cold. If he ties us up and leaves us here, we'll freeze to death, she thought. She had to come up with a plan, and fast.

Their captor was coming toward them, the rope in one hand and the gun in the other. As he prepared to tie them up, he grasped the rope with his other hand, relaxing his grip on the gun for a split second.

Nancy sensed her opening and used it. She lunged forward, knocking the gun out of his hand and sending it bouncing and skittering across the open space of the warehouse. "Run!" she screamed to Bess, but her friend was frozen to the spot.

Rubbing his wrist, the man moved menacingly toward them. "I can take care of you even without a gun," he said, backing them up against the door to the civet pen.

Reaching behind her for something to hold him off, Nancy made a discovery—the door to the civet cage was unlocked! As the man's hands reached toward her throat, she ducked under his arms and darted forward, pulling the cage door open.

The terrified civets burst out, yelping and howling.

Nancy grabbed Bess's arm and dragged her to the door of the warehouse, pushing her roughly into the street. Then she turned back, just in time to see one of the civets leaping at the man's face.

After she ran out, Nancy slammed the door shut behind her. Bess was already in the car. Nancy jumped into the passenger seat, and they roared off.

"Stop at the next phone booth," Nancy said after they'd gotten a few blocks away. When Bess did, Nancy leapt out and called the River Heights police.

"I told them where they could find the stolen civets," she told Bess as she got back in. "The man with sunglasses will probably get away, though."

Bess took a deep, shaky breath. "I've never been so scared in my life," she admitted. "I really didn't think we were going to get out of there."

"Well, we did," Nancy said, reaching over and giving her a hug. "And I'll tell you one thing—I'm positive Owen had nothing to do with this. He would never let the civets be treated so badly."

Bess nodded. "I still want to know what he was doing with Zoe, though."

"There's got to be some explanation," Nancy concluded. "First, though, we'd better get back to the zoo. I think it's time to confront Zoe Spelios once and for all."

Bess agreed, then Nancy had another thought. "Hang on a second. I want to call George and warn her to stay away from the zoo."

"Good idea. But make it quick. If that guy gets away before the police arrive, he'll go straight to Zoe. Now that we're on to them, they may get desperate."

Nancy nodded, jumped back out of the car, and dialed George's number. Mrs. Fayne answered the phone.

"I'm sorry, Nancy, she's not here," Mrs. Fayne told her. "She went to the zoo with Owen. They said something about talking to Mr. Berry. You just missed them."

"Thanks." Nancy said goodbye and hung up. Then she jumped back in the car. "I think we'd better get to the zoo right away," she told Bess. "George and Owen are on their way there."

"They don't know about any of this!" Bess cried. "They could be in serious danger." She bore down on the accelerator.

Nancy and Bess sped to the zoo, parking in the visitors' part of the lot to avoid running into Zoe in the staff lot.

"How on earth are we going to get in?" Bess wailed. "There are security guards all over the place, and they know we're not allowed in."

"Let's see if they recognize us," Nancy suggested. "Maybe we can get away with it." They walked casually up to the gate and peered into the security booth. No luck! The guard on duty was none other than Harper Anderson.

"Duck!" Nancy said quickly as he swung around in their direction. The two girls darted under the guardhouse window.

As they were creeping away from the guardhouse, Nancy noticed a yellow school bus about fifty yards from the gate. A class of high school students was piling out of the bus into the parking lot.

Talking and laughing, the students headed for the gate. "Know any of them?" Nancy asked Bess.

"I don't think so," she answered, puzzled.

"We do now," Nancy told her. Taking her arm, they ran into the middle of the group of students.

"Hi, I'm Nancy," she said to a cute boy with curly black hair. "Mind if I go in with you?"

The boy looked at her, then looked up at the sky. "Hallelujah, my prayers are answered!" he said with a smile.

Taking her cue from Nancy, Bess attached herself to a slim, athletic-looking redheaded boy in a green ski jacket. "Nice jacket. I bet you're a skier," she said breathlessly.

"I play soccer, actually," he said. He looked at her appreciatively. "But I'll go skiing with you anytime."

Still flirting with the guys, Nancy and Bess walked through the gate in the middle of the group of teenagers. Harper didn't even look up as they went by.

As soon as they got inside, Nancy turned to her escort. "I've got to go now," she said quickly. "But thanks."

"That had to be the world's shortest date," he said, shrugging good-naturedly.

Bess said to her soccer player, "It's been nice knowing you."

"Where to?" Bess asked after they were safely inside the zoo.

"The main administration building," Nancy told her. "That's where Mr. Berry's office is."

Then Nancy stopped dead in her tracks. "Look, there are Zoe and Tyler!" she whispered excitedly.

"Where are they going?" Bess whispered back. Zoe and Tyler were walking away from the World of Africa building. As the girls watched, they turned down a deserted-looking path.

"Let's go," Bess said, but Nancy shook her head no.

"They'll see us," she explained. The trees along the path were leafless, giving them no place to hide.

"We can't just let them get away!" Bess protested. "We've got to find out what they're doing!"

Nancy nodded. Then the Sky Ride, the aerial tramway that took visitors across the zoo, caught her attention. As she watched, a gondola passed directly over the path Zoe and Tyler were taking.

"I'll take the tramway," she told Bess. "You go and find Owen and George. Let them know what's happening. Be careful, and tell Mr. Berry, too."

Bess nodded. "Let's meet back at World of Africa."

As Bess ran off, Nancy sprinted to the entrance of the Sky Ride. There was a line of people waiting to get on the tramway, and some of them complained loudly as she pushed through to the front.

"Hey, what do you think you're doing?" one man called to her. "There's a line here, you know."

The ride operator didn't want to let Nancy get

on the ride. "It's an emergency," she protested, but no one was listening. Her heart sank.

Then she spotted the curly-haired guy who had been her "date" when she entered the zoo. He was at the very front of the line.

"I'm with him," she said loudly. "There you are, honey," she said desperately, waving and smiling.

To her relief he waved back. "I thought you'd never get here!" he called. Still grumbling, the crowd opened to let her through.

"Sorry about that," she said to the curly-haired boy as they hopped on the next gondola. The car swung up and over the trees, swaying a little in the icy wind.

"Now that we're dating, you could at least tell me your name," he answered, smiling.

"Nancy Drew," she said, holding out her hand.

He shook it. "Bob Bannister," he replied.

Turning her attention to the scene below, Nancy quickly spotted Tyler and Zoe. They seemed to be arguing about something. As the gondola passed closer, Nancy leaned down to hear what they were saying.

The zookeeper's voice was too soft to be heard, but Tyler was almost shouting. "It's not enough, I tell you! You must have more!"

More what? Nancy wondered. Before she could find out, the gondola passed by. She twisted in the chair, causing it to rock dangerously, but Tyler and Zoe were out of sight.

"Looking for someone?" Bob Bannister asked, holding on to the side of the gondola as she rocked it.

Nancy was about to answer when, with a sharp jab, she felt something like a rock hit her arm. She looked down, startled.

Sticking out of the sleeve of her ski jacket was a long, ugly-looking dart!

Chapter

Fifteen

NANCY GASPED and recoiled instinctively.

"Are you all right?" Bob Bannister asked.

She nodded, pulling the dart out of her sleeve. "Just a little shook up," she told him, shaking herself. "Luckily it didn't hit my skin."

Nancy breathed a sigh of relief. If it hadn't been for the padding of her ski jacket, the dart would have sunk deep into her arm.

Taking a closer look at the dart, Nancy saw it was long and sharp. In an instant she remembered where she'd seen one like it before.

"A tranquilizer dart," she murmured, a wave of fear washing over her. Who knows what effect a tranquilizer meant for animals could have on a human being?

"You have dangerous friends, Nancy Drew," said Bob, raising an eyebrow at the vicious-looking dart.

"Dangerous enemies, you mean," she corrected him. She carefully placed the dart inside one of her ski gloves and put the glove in her jacket pocket.

Craning her neck, Nancy looked back in the direction where the dart had come from. Tyler and Zoe were still out of sight, but Nancy thought she caught a glimpse of Tyler's red hair.

Whoever shot her was clearly desperate, Nancy realized. Was it the zookeeper, or had the man with the sunglasses come after her?

Either way, she thought, we're all in danger, and there isn't a thing I can do about it from up here! The gondola was beginning its descent, but it moved painfully slowly. Even worse—as long as she was up in the air, she was a sitting duck!

As they descended, they passed a tree whose branches scraped against the gondola. "This is where I get off," she told Bob. Before he could reply, she grabbed a thick branch and swung out of the car.

Nancy hung in midair for one long, agonizing moment. Then she managed to clasp her legs around the branch and slide to safety, scratching her gloveless hand.

Swiftly she climbed down the trunk of the tree, sliding the last ten feet to the ground. She landed hard and temporarily lost her balance. Then she managed to steady herself by grabbing the tree.

Realizing she'd need proof to back any of her theories, Nancy decided to head for Zoe's office, and fast. She ran down the path where she had last seen Tyler and Zoe. It came out near the snack bar, across from the World of Africa. The zookeeper was nowhere in sight, and Nancy was about to head for the staff entrance when she saw Bess, Owen, and George approaching from the other direction.

She ran up to them. "Things are getting dangerous," she said. "Someone just tried to shoot me with a tranquilizer dart."

Bess gasped. "Nancy, your hand is bleeding!"

She glanced down. "I'll put something on it later. Right now I've got to get to Zoe's office."

"What for?" George asked. She'd looked concerned at first, but her expression grew cold when Nancy mentioned Zoe. "Nobody's asking you to work on the case anymore," she added icily.

"But, George, we know who's been stealing the civets!" Nancy said excitedly. "Didn't Bess tell you?"

"I just found them a minute ago," Bess said quickly. "I haven't told them anything yet."

"Well, I know it wasn't Owen," Nancy told them, turning to him with an embarrassed smile.

"I really owe you an apology," she said honestly. "I was following Zoe yesterday, and when she met you at the drugstore, I didn't know what to think—"

"So you assumed he was guilty," George finished for her in the same icy tone. "When he was actually just asking her to reconsider her decision about letting him work at the zoo."

"What I still don't understand is why you had that dart gun," Nancy said, turning to Owen.

Owen said, "You must mean the gun I had in the car. Zoe asked me to pick up a replacement for the stolen civet at the airport, and gave me a tranquilizer gun in case the shot it had been given for the trip had worn off. When I got fired, I gave the gun back to her."

"So you thought—" George started furiously.

"George, it was an honest mistake," Bess cut in. Her voice had a pleading tone. "You know Nancy was only trying to help."

"Thanks, but we can do without that kind of help," George said. Without looking at Nancy, she turned and walked away. Owen ran after her.

Nancy felt as though someone had poured cold water on her. Bess shrugged helplessly. "I tried talking to them, but they won't listen," she said. "George is still furious because you tailed Owen."

"I'm sorry she feels that way, but I have to crack this case," Nancy said, pushing her hurt feelings aside. "Our lives may be in danger! Whether George likes it or not, I can't just walk away."

Taking a deep breath, Nancy followed George with her eyes. How could she convince her best friend that she only had her interests at heart? It didn't look as if George was going to listen to reason, and time was running out.

"Look," Nancy said, turning to Bess, "I have to check out Zoe's office. Would you mind keeping an eye on George? I'm afraid of what might happen if Zoe comes after her or Owen."

Bess nodded. "I'll do my best. And, Nancy," she added, "I'm behind you." When Nancy still didn't move, she felt Bess give her a little push. "Go on. The best way to get George back is to solve the case," she pointed out.

Bess went after George and Owen, while Nancy dashed down the path to the staff entrance. Luckily the door was open. After searching the empty reception area, Nancy slipped into Zoe's office.

The zookeeper seemed to have run out in a hurry—a lab coat was draped on top of a coat rack in one corner, and several hangers lay on the floor.

Nancy went to Zoe's bookcase and picked up the photograph of Jacques Mathieu. When she looked carefully at it, she realized the photo wasn't the same one that appeared in *Fit for a Queen*. In that picture Mathieu had been wearing a dark suit, while in Zoe's photograph he had on white Bermuda shorts and a sweater.

Also, in Zoe's picture Mathieu wasn't alone. There were two children seated at his feet, a boy and a girl.

Both children were dark-haired and handsome. Nancy quickly removed the frame and looked at the back of the photograph. Someone had written in the date—twenty-five years ago. That would make the children about thirty now, Nancy guessed.

Still looking for clues that would connect the zookeeper with the civet thefts, Nancy went through Zoe's desk drawers. In the back of a bottom drawer she hit pay dirt—a pile of stationery with the Classic Scents logo!

She tried the other drawers. Most contained papers relating to zoo business, but one small drawer was locked.

Nancy found a paper clip, which she untwisted and slid into the lock. It clicked open almost immediately.

She pulled the drawer out. Inside was a manila folder labeled *Propriété de J. Mathieu.*

Property of Jacques Mathieu, she translated to herself from the French. She opened the folder and found that it held some yellowing sheets of paper covered with crabbed writing. *Recette trois,* she read off one. Nancy frowned. Recipes? But for what?

Leafing through the pages, she came on one that made her draw in her breath. "Recipe for Belle Soirée," she read aloud. The recipes were perfume formulas—including one for the lost fragrance!

After looking through all the papers, Nancy replaced them in the envelope. As she was putting it back in the drawer, her hand hit something hard.

She felt around in the drawer, finally locating a small velvet bag. Inside was a glittering crystal flacon labeled Belle Soirée!

The police will need to see this piece of evidence, she thought, putting the flacon in her pocket.

Nancy knew she had to call them fast—Zoe could come back at any moment! She reached for the telephone, but before she could call, she heard a strange noise coming from a corner of the room.

"Unnhhh!" It was a man's voice. Nancy jumped as she heard the groan again. "Ummph!"

She glanced around and saw a door in the far wall, probably a closet. The sound seemed to be coming from there.

"Help!" The man groaned, more audibly this time. He was definitely in the closet. Nancy rushed over and turned the knob, but the door was locked.

"Who's in there?" she called softly.

The man didn't seem to hear her. "Some-ummph help!" he called.

Nancy looked around desperately for a way to force the door. Then she remembered seeing a credit card among the paraphernalia in Zoe's desk drawer.

She ran back to the desk, found the card, and fitted it between the closet door and door frame. It slid in easily, but before she could spring the lock, she heard footsteps coming along the passageway.

Stuffing the credit card into her pocket, Nancy glanced wildly around the room in search of a hiding place. As the footsteps came closer, she flung herself across the room and crouched behind the coat rack.

A second later Zoe came in, speaking rapidly in French. From her hiding place Nancy could still see that behind Zoe was the man with the sunglasses.

Nancy covered her mouth with her hand to keep from gasping out loud. The man was wearing a bandage on his face, probably from the civet scratches. Somehow he had managed to escape before the police came—and now she was trapped just a few feet from him!

Still talking, Zoe pulled out a key and unlocked the door to the closet. As it swung open, she took a dart gun out of her pocket and pointed it at whoever was inside.

"Don't shoot!" the man begged, staggering out of the closet and into the room. He was holding his chin, which was beginning to show a large, ugly bruise.

Nancy gasped again, her head whirling with surprise and fear. The man was Tyler Mack!

Chapter
Sixteen

TYLER FELL into the middle of the room. "Don't hit me again!" he begged. "I won't talk, I swear!"

Nancy leaned forward, straining to see through the forest of coats. So Tyler and Zoe weren't accomplices after all! Nancy gently pulled back the edge of a coat. She just had to hear what was going on.

The man in the sunglasses said coldly to Tyler, "Thanks to your meddling, you've learned too much about Classic Scents. We can't afford to let you go free."

Tyler's eyes bulged as the man's implication became clear. "What—what are you going to do with me?"

The man smiled. "I don't know yet. You might make a nice meal for the polar bears—"

"Jean!" Zoe said sternly. "We don't have time for this nonsense!"

"Or maybe I'll just shoot you," Jean finished. He pointed to the gun. "This may look like a simple tranquilizer gun, but I've filled the darts with a lethal poison."

Tyler gasped. "You wouldn't use it!"

"Oh, but I would," Jean assured him. "In fact, I've already used it. I just took care of the ringleader of those teenage brats who found the civets."

Nancy swayed slightly. So it was Jean who had shot at her—and the dart had contained a deadly poison! She'd been only millimeters from death!

Tyler stared from Jean to the poison dart gun, his eyes darting back and forth in abject terror.

As Nancy watched, something inside Tyler seemed to crack. *"No!"* he screamed, lunging desperately at Jean in an attempt to get the gun.

There was a faint *pfft* sound, and Tyler fell to the ground, clutching his stomach. Zoe gave a little shriek. "You imbecile, you've ruined everything!" she cried to Jean. *"Now* what will we do with him?"

"We'll take him with us," Jean replied coolly.

"To New York?" Zoe wailed.

"That won't be necessary. We'll dump him on the way to the airport." Jean leaned over to pick up Tyler's unconscious body, which had fallen dangerously near Nancy's hiding place. She squeezed farther behind the coats, praying he wouldn't notice her.

"He's still breathing," Jean continued. "The poison takes several hours to work, but with luck no one will find him before then."

"Wrap his head in something," Zoe commanded. "That red hair is visible a mile away."

Jean looked around for something to put on Tyler's head. Nancy cringed as his eye fell on the lab coat hanging over her hiding place.

"This should do the trick," he said, whipping it off the hook and leaving Nancy with nowhere to hide.

With a burst of fear, she kicked out, hoping to disarm Jean before he realized what was going on. The gun flew across the room, but Jean grabbed her and twisted her arm behind her back.

"Well, look who's here, the girl detective," he said. "You're hard to shake, aren't you?"

Her heart pounding, Nancy desperately tried to loosen her captor's grip. Before she could break free, Zoe retrieved the gun from the corner where it had landed and pointed it straight at her.

"Don't try anything," she said grimly. "I would be very happy to kill you."

Jean let her go, and slowly Nancy put her hands up. "I see I missed you in the gondola," he said. When she nodded, he added, "Well, I won't miss now. You've caused us enough trouble."

"Thanks to you and your friends, the civets have escaped," Zoe spat out angrily. "We'll have to start all over again."

"You mean you don't have enough civet oil yet to manufacture Belle Soirée?" Nancy asked. She took the crystal flacon out of her pocket, holding it out so Zoe could see it. "That *is* what you plan to do, isn't it—use the stolen formula to make Jacques Mathieu's perfume?"

For a moment Zoe looked shocked. Then her face twisted into a smile. "You're a lot smarter than I gave you credit for," she said. "You've been a thorn in my side since the day I met you."

"Yes, she's been very intelligent," Jean agreed. "Too bad she won't get to use those brains any longer."

He took the gun back from Zoe and motioned Nancy to walk out the door of the office ahead of him. "We can't take you with us, and you're not worth wasting another dart on. So I've decided to let nature take its course."

Jean turned to Zoe. "The snake is still in the holding room, isn't it?" She nodded. "I'll put her in there."

A wave of panic washed over Nancy as Jean pushed her toward the door next to Zoe's office. Driven by fear, she made a wild attempt to twist her arms free, but he only laughed and gripped her tighter.

"You know what's in there, don't you?" he said, smiling with evil pleasure. "Zoe told me that the snake in this room has a bite more lethal than ten poison darts. People who get bitten die within minutes."

Nancy's blood ran cold at the casual way he described it. Jean continued, "No one will ever be able to pin your death on us. It will simply look like your snooping got you in trouble—for one last time."

"How—" Nancy began, but he motioned her to be quiet. "Zoe, give me the key to the room." Zoe complied, totally willing to let Jean give the orders. "Now go and guard the hallway. That way you won't have to watch."

As Zoe left, Jean explained, "Zoe always found violence hard to take. Even when we were children."

"When you were together in France, you mean?" Nancy asked.

"Exactly," Jean told her. "Zoe is my little cousin," he explained. "And soon the Mathieu cousins will be together again, making perfume and getting rich in New York."

He paused. "First, though, I need to get rid of you." Carefully he opened the door to the holding room. "Walk inside. Now!" he barked when she hesitated.

Jean pushed her ahead of him into the room. The African cobra was coiled in a small pen in one corner, watching them warily. The room's temperature had been adjusted to resemble its native desert, and Nancy felt herself starting to sweat.

"The snake is hungry today," Jean whispered. "Zoe said they only feed it once a week."

As Nancy watched in horror, Jean threw a rock at the motionless snake. It hissed a little and lifted its head, swaying slightly from side to side.

Jean threw a second rock, and the cobra reared up into striking position. Its forked tongue flicked swiftly in and out, and the hooded head seemed to grow larger.

Nancy felt herself go rigid with fear. The snake opened its mouth and hissed loudly, revealing long white fangs. Still holding Nancy with his right hand, Jean reached forward and unlatched the door of the pen with his left.

Sensing danger, the snake struck out. With a final shove Jean pushed Nancy straight toward its lethal fangs!

Chapter

Seventeen

NANCY STUMBLED FORWARD into the pen and nearly fell over the angry cobra. Unable to redirect its strike, the snake shot past her, sinking its fangs harmlessly into the side of the wooden pen.

Hissing furiously, the cobra freed itself and reared up again. With desperate strength Nancy pushed off with her left foot and leapt backward out of the pen.

She crashed into Jean, striking out wildly with her fists as she fell. He grunted in pain at the unexpected assault and struck savagely at her with the dart gun.

As he raised the gun to hit her again, Nancy managed to twist it away from him. Jean grabbed at her arm, but she kicked him hard in the stomach until he loosened his grip.

The snake hissed loudly from behind her, and she realized that it was about to strike again. As it shot forward she spun around and pumped a dart into it, hitting it squarely in the middle of the head.

The snake kept coming for a second, then dropped, limply, at Nancy's feet. Swiftly she turned back and trained the gun on Jean.

The Frenchman's face was contorted with anger. He started to lunge at her, then paused as a scream came echoing down the hallway.

"Jean! Help!"

"Zoe!" Before Nancy could stop him, he ran out the door in the direction of the scream. With a last look at the cobra, Nancy followed.

The scene in the hallway was chaotic. Owen and George were holding Zoe. Bess was screaming at the zookeeper. "Where's Nancy? What have you done to her?"

Jean came running out and hit Owen in the stomach, knocking him to the ground. He tried to pull Zoe away, but George wouldn't let go of her arm. "Tell me where Nancy is!" she shouted. "Where's my friend?"

"I'm right here, George," Nancy called back, running down the hall. She pointed the dart gun at Zoe and Jean, shouting, "One more move and I'll shoot! Put your hands up!"

Owen got up from the floor as the civet thieves

slowly complied. "I'll call the police," he said faintly.

"I think you'd better," Nancy agreed. "These two have got a lot of talking to do."

"Nancy, I'm sorry. I should never have accused you of not caring," George said sheepishly. It was late the next morning, and she and Nancy were sitting in George's living room, waiting for Owen and Bess to arrive. They were going to the zoo to talk to Maurice Berry about getting Owen his job back.

"I really flew off the handle, didn't I?" George continued.

"And I jumped to conclusions. I should have trusted your judgment more," Nancy admitted.

"No, you did the right thing," George said decidedly. "Owen's behavior did look suspicious, but I'm awfully glad it wasn't," she added.

"So am I," said Nancy sincerely. "He's a great guy."

The doorbell rang, and Owen and Bess came in. "Owen gave me a lift over," Bess explained. "Phew! Your house still smells like perfume!"

"It's hard to believe the party was less than a week ago," Nancy said as they returned to the living room. "It seems like months."

"You guys never told us what happened at the station house," Bess said. Nancy and Owen had gone with the police the night before when they came to arrest Jean and Zoe.

"Jean was pretty tight lipped, but Zoe confessed right away," Nancy said. "It turns out Jacques Mathieu was their grandfather. When he died she discovered the formula for Belle Soirée among his papers, but instead of turning it over to the company that had bought his company and rightfully owned it, she decided to reproduce the fragrance and market it herself."

Nancy shuddered, remembering Zoe's twisted expression as she told the story. The zookeeper had been nearly hysterical. "Apparently, she really believed that the formula was rightfully hers. So she enlisted her cousin Jean to help her."

"He's the spitting image of his grandfather Jacques Mathieu," Bess said. "Why were they stealing the civets and not just buying the oil?"

"Zoe was afraid other perfume makers would notice if she bought the oil from the regular suppliers," Nancy explained. "There are only two or three of them, and it seemed risky to her. So when she heard that the River Heights Zoo was starting a civet colony, she applied for a job there."

"Don't tell me she wasn't really a zookeeper!" Owen asked in surprise. "She seemed to know what she was doing."

"No, she really was a zookeeper," Nancy told him. "She said she loved animals."

"Then how could she allow them to be treated so badly?" Bess burst out. "That warehouse was awful."

"She said she didn't know," Nancy said. "Jean insisted on handling all those details."

"And he was completely cold-blooded," Bess said with a shudder. "Look how many times he tried to kill you!"

Nancy nodded. "And he could have killed Tyler," she reminded them grimly. "It seems that Tyler found out about the civets and saw his chance to make some quick cash. He was blackmailing Zoe, so Jean decided to get rid of him."

"Unbelievable." Owen shook his head. "And I thought the only things zoologists had to worry about were wild animals!"

The others laughed. "Speaking of which, we'd better get over to the zoo," Nancy said. "Mr. Berry asked us to be there by noon."

George and Owen drove to the zoo together in Owen's car, while Bess went with Nancy in the Mustang. As they were approaching the entrance, Bess asked, "Will they let us in?"

"They should," Nancy replied, smiling. "Still, let's park in the staff lot, just in case."

Owen parked next to Nancy, and the four of them walked across the lot to the back gate. "It all looks so harmless during the day," Bess marveled.

"Especially now that Jean and Zoe are behind bars," George agreed.

When they arrived at Maurice Berry's office, the director stood up to greet them. "Please accept my apologies," he said. "You should be very proud of yourselves," he continued. "You've done us a great service."

"Nancy was the brains of the operation," Bess said loyally. "We just helped."

Mr. Berry turned to Nancy. "I'm glad to find out first-hand that your reputation is so well deserved," he told her. "Thank you again."

Nancy smiled—it always felt great to solve a case. "I was glad to help," she said honestly.

The phone rang in Mr. Berry's office, and the others waited while he answered it. There was a long silence as he listened to the person on the other end. Then he said, "Oh, good. Thanks very much for calling."

"That was the hospital. Tyler is going to be all right," he announced, hanging up the receiver. "They got him there in time and administered an antidote to the poison."

"What happens to him after he's recovered?" Bess asked.

"I don't know. He certainly won't be working here," Mr. Berry told her. "We need to find two new zookeepers for World of Africa."

He smiled at Owen. "I wish you were graduating this year, Mr. Harris. I'd hire you in a second."

Owen beamed. George asked, "Does this mean he can continue working on his project?"

"Absolutely," Mr. Berry confirmed. He turned

to Owen. "I'll even speak to your college about a second internship this summer, if you're interested."

"So you'd be around all summer!" George said, her eyes shining.

"I'd love it. Thank you, sir," Owen said, returning George's smile.

"Can we go see the civets now?" Bess asked. "I'm so glad the police found all of them!"

"A little the worse for wear, but they're adjusting well," Mr. Berry said. He walked them to World of Africa, where all ten civets were scampering about in their special environment.

Owen, George, Nancy, and Bess watched with delight as the civets wrestled playfully near the front of the enclosure. "They're so cute," George said with a sigh. "It's hard to believe anyone would mistreat them."

"Or that they smell so bad," Bess added, wrinkling her nose. She turned to Owen. "You'd better be careful you don't pick it up, working with them. I don't want my cousin dating a skunk!"

Owen laughed and planted a kiss on George's nose. "You don't need to worry about that!"

Suddenly Nancy snapped her fingers. "Oh, I forgot! Speaking of smells—" She reached into her handbag and pulled out a little glass vial. She handed it to Bess, saying, "I thought you'd like to have this."

Bess unstoppered the vial and sniffed it, then

squealed with delight. "Nancy, this is Belle Soirée! Where did you get it?"

Nancy smiled at her friend's excitement. "I found it in Zoe's office. I don't think she'll have much use for it in prison."

"Oh, thank you!" Bess dabbed some on her wrists and neck and offered it to the others. "Anyone?"

"Phew, what is that?" Owen waved his hand in front of his nose. "It reeks in here!"

"This is the most famous and expensive perfume in the whole world," Bess told him, exaggerating slightly. "It's made from civet oil."

"I'd rather smell like the civet!" Owen exclaimed, holding his nose.

The others laughed, and after a minute a reluctant Bess joined in. "Men!" she huffed. "You have no taste." Then, as George looked daggers at her, she added, "In perfume! You have no taste in perfume!"

Nancy's next case:

When waitress Cynthia Tyler is accused of stealing and is fired from the popular restaurant Touchdown, Nancy goes undercover to find out why. She discovers a connection between the missing money and several members of the Bedford High football team—including Cynthia's boyfriend, star quarterback Rob Matthews.

Someone is willing to play very rough to keep Nancy from intercepting the truth behind the Bedford High scandal. The players take their football seriously—far too seriously for their own good. On the field, they break all the rules of good sportsmanship and good health. Off the field, they have joined in a shady deal that could send the game into sudden death . . . in *OUT OF BOUNDS,* Case #45 in the Nancy Drew Files™.